SWEEP #8

Changeling

Cate Tiernan

PUFFIN BOOKS

All quoted materials in this work were created by the author.
Any resemblance to existing works is accidental.

Changeling

Puffin Books
Published by the Penguin Group
Penguin Putnam Books for Young Readers,
345 Hudson Street, New York, New York 10014, U.S.A.
Penguin Books Ltd, 80 Strand, London WC2R 0RL, England
Penguin Books Australia Ltd, Ringwood, Victoria, Australia
Penguin Books Canada Ltd, 10 Alcorn Avenue, Toronto, Ontario, Canada M4V 3B2
Penguin Books (N.Z.) Ltd, 182-190 Wairau Road, Auckland 10, New Zealand

Penguin Books Ltd, Registered Offices: Harmondsworth, Middlesex, England

Published by Puffin Books,
a division of Penguin Putnam Books for Young Readers, 2001

1 3 5 7 9 10 8 6 4 2

Cover photography by Michael Heissner/Stone and Jim Stamates/Stone
Photo-illustration by Marci Senders
Series design by Russell Gordon

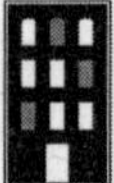

Produced by 17th Street Productions,
an Alloy Online, Inc. company
151 West 26th Street
New York, NY 10001

ISBN 0-14-230057-8

Printed in the United States of America

To my inner wolf.

1. Breakthrough

Surely I did not know the meaning of the word Godforsaken until I arrived at this place. Barra Head is on the westernmost shore of the highlands of Scotland, and a wilder, more untamed countryside it would be difficult to imagine. Yet, Brother Colin, how exalted I am to be here, how eager to bring the Lord's message to these good people. Tomorrow I shall set forth among the inhabitants, taking to them the joy of the Word of God.

—Brother Sinestus Tor, Cistercian monk, in a letter to his brother Colin, also a monk, September 1767

"Okay, I'm gone," said my sister, Mary K., whirling to run downstairs. We'd just heard the distinctive horn beep of her friend Jaycee's mom's minivan.

"See you," I called after her. Although Mary K. was my little sister, she was fourteen going on twenty-five, and in some ways, like for instance her chest, she looked more mature than I did.

"Honey?" My mom poked her head around my bedroom door. "Please come with us to Eileen and Paula's."

"Oh, no thanks," I said, trying not to sound rude. I loved my aunt Eileen and her girlfriend, Paula, but I couldn't face having to interact with them, smile, eat, pretend everything was normal—when only days ago my entire life had split at the seams.

"She's made seaweed salad," Mom said temptingly.

"Augh!" I crossed my two index fingers to ward off health food, and my mom made a face.

"Okay. Just thought you'd want to have a last family meal," she said in her best guilt-inducing voice.

"Mom, you'll only be gone eleven days. I'll know you for the rest of my life. Plenty of family meals in our future," I said. The next day my parents were leaving on a cruise to the Bahamas, to celebrate their twenty-fifth wedding anniversary.

"Mary Grace?" my dad called. Translated that meant, "get a move on."

"Okay." Mom looked at me speculatively, and suddenly all the humor in the situation was gone. My parents and I had been through a lot in the past couple of months, and every once in a while the memories came back to bite us.

"Have a good time," I said, turning away. "Say hi to Eileen and Paula."

"Mary Grace?" my dad said again. "Bye, Morgan. We won't be late."

Once I heard the front door close, I felt my shoulders sag in relief. Alone at last. Free to be myself, at least for a little while. Free to feel miserable, to lie curled on my bed, to wander the house aimlessly without having to talk to anyone or try to look normal.

Free to be myself. That was a joke. The *me* that was Wiccan.

Not only Wiccan, but a blood witch and a Woodbane—the most infamous of Wicca's Seven Great Clans. The *me* whose biological father, Ciaran MacEwan, had killed my birth mother, Maeve Riordan. Ciaran was one of the most evil, dangerous, remorseless witches there was, and half of me came from him. So what did that say about me?

I looked at myself in my bedroom mirror. I still *looked* like me: straight brown hair, brownish hazel eyes, a tiny bit tilted at the corner, strong nose. I was five-six, seventeen years old, and had yet to develop a feminine curve anywhere on my body.

I didn't look like a Rowlands. For sixteen years I had never once thought I wasn't a Rowlands, despite looking different from the rest of my family, despite the huge differences between Mary K and me. Now we all knew why those differences existed. Because I had been born a Riordan.

I dropped onto my bed, my chest aching. Only days ago I had narrowly escaped death—Ciaran had tried to kill me in Manhattan. Only at the last minute, when he'd realized that I was his daughter, had Ciaran changed his mind and allowed my then boyfriend, Hunter Niall, to save me. My father was a man who had killed my mother. Who had tried to kill *me*. Ciaran was evil beyond belief, and that evil was part of me. How could Hunter even pretend not to understand why I had broken up with him?

Oh, Goddess, Hunter, I thought, filled with longing. I loved him, I lusted after him, I admired and trusted and respected him. He was tall, blond, gorgeous, and had a fabulous English accent. He was a powerful, initiated blood witch, half Woodbane, and he was a Seeker for the International Council of Witches. He was my mùirn beatha dàn—my soul mate. For most people, that meant they were supposed to be together forever.

But I was descended from one of the worst witches in Wiccan history. My very blood was tainted forever. I was poison; I would destroy anything I touched. I couldn't bear to hurt Hunter, couldn't bear to even take the chance that I would. So I had told him I didn't love him anymore. I'd told him to leave me alone.

Which was why I was alone now, having spent the last few days clutching a pillow, aching with loneliness, and sick with misery.

"What can I do?" I asked myself. It was Saturday, and my coven, Kithic, would be meeting as usual for a circle. One of our eight annual Sabbats, Imbolc, was coming up soon, and I knew we would be starting to talk about it and preparing to celebrate it. Going to a circle, making the commitment to observe every week, was part of the pattern of Wiccan life. It was part of the turning of the Wheel of the Year, part of learning. I knew I should go.

But I knew I couldn't. Couldn't bear seeing Hunter. Couldn't bear seeing the other people in my circle, having them look at me with sympathy, fear, or distrust.

"Meow?"

I looked down at my kitten.

"Dagda," I said, picking him up. "You're turning into a big boy. You have a big meow." I stroked Dagda, feeling his rumbly purr.

If I went to the circle tonight, I would have to see Hunter, feel his eyes on me, hear his voice. Would I be strong enough to face that? I didn't think so.

"I can't go," I told Dagda. "I won't. I'll make a circle here." I got up, feeling that this was a way to keep my commitment to observe the Wiccan circle. Maybe drawing on the power would help my pain. Maybe it would take my mind off Hunter and off my own inherent evil, at least for a little while.

I went to the back of my closet and brought my altar out from under my bathrobe. As far as I knew, my parents hadn't discovered it yet. It was a small footlocker, covered with a violet linen cloth, and I used it in the rites I did at home. It was hidden in the back of my closet, where it wouldn't be noticed by my devoutly Catholic parents. To them, it was bad enough that I practiced Wicca at all, and they would be really, really unhappy if they knew I had all this witch stuff in their house.

I shoved the footlocker into the middle of the room, aligning its four corners with the four points of the compass. (I had figured this out weeks ago and memorized the position it should be in.) On each of the four corners of the footlocker I set the silver ceremonial bowls that had belonged to my birth mother. As always, I looked at them with love and appreciation. I had never known Maeve—I had been only seven months old when Ciaran killed her—but I had her witch's tools, and they meant everything to me.

Into one bowl I put fresh water. In one bowl half full of sand I stuck an incense stick and lit it. The thin gray stream of scented smoke symbolized air. Another bowl held a handful of stones and crystals, to symbolize earth. In the last bowl I lit a thick red candle, for fire. The candle was red for power, for passion, for fire, for me. Fire was my element: I scried with fire; I could summon fire at will.

I quickly shed my clothes and got into my green robe. The silk was thin and embroidered with ancient Celtic signs, runes, sigils of protection and power. Maeve had worn this, leading circles for her coven, Belwicket, back in Ireland. Her mother, Mackenna, had worn it before her. And so on, for generations. I loved wearing it, knowing I was fulfilling my destiny, feeling a connection with women I had never known. Could Maeve's goodness cancel out Ciaran's evil? Which half would win in me?

As the folds flowed around me, encasing me with their magickal vibrations, I took out my other tools: a ceremonial dagger called an athame and a witch's wand, long, slim, and decorated with lines of silver beaten into the dark, old wood. I was ready.

First I drew a circle on my floor with chalk. With fleeting pride, I noticed that my circle-drawing was getting much better. It was now nearly perfect. I stepped in, closed the circle, and knelt before my altar. "Goddess and God, I call on thee," I said softly, looking into my candle's flame. "Your daughter Morgan calls on your goodness and your power. Help me make magick. Help me learn. Show me what I am ready to know." Closing my eyes, I let out all my breath, then slowly drew it in again. Within a minute I was deeply into meditation: I had practiced so much that meditation was like using a muscle. It was there, it was almost immediate, and it was strong.

What am I ready to know? I asked. In my mind a narrow road unspooled before me. Trees and shrubs lined each side, making the road both inviting and secluded. I moved down the road, smoothly and with no sense of pace—as if I were floating above the hard-packed earth. It felt wonderful, exciting. Eagerly I sped forward.

I flew around a curve and then recoiled in sudden horror, a wordless scream coming from my mouth. Before me, blocking my way, was a dying serpent, a black, roiling, two-headed snake. Its flesh was hacked and eaten away; acrid blood stained the roadbed, its bitter, repugnant scent making me cover my nose and mouth. The thing was dying. It curled upon itself in agony, twisting as it lost its breath and felt its blood flow. I backed up slowly, not sure how dangerous it still was, and then from the sky a beautiful, cold, crystalline cage dropped over the thing. With one last shriek of torment the two-headed black serpent lashed its barbed tail and died. The cage shimmered over it gently, seeming made of air, of music, of gold, of crystal. It was made of magick. I had made it. And my cage had helped kill the serpent.

Gasping, I clawed my way back to consciousness, opening my eyes to find my heart pounding, the scent of the serpent's blood still in my throat. I wanted to gag, the horrible images still behind my eyes. The serpent had been Cal Blaire and Selene Belltower. It didn't take a psychology major to figure that one out. My subconscious was obviously still working through that particular horror. The deaths of Cal, the first boy I had ever loved, and his mother, Selene, a powerful, dark Woodbane witch, were still ever present in my everyday awareness. I gazed at my red candle and shuddered. There was no way I could explore that path any more tonight. Maybe I needed to see it, maybe magick had needed me to see something, learn something, but I couldn't face it. I hoped that with the passage of time, the memory would sink deeper.

I swallowed and watched the scented smoke rise from the incense. Maybe if I had continued down the road of my subconscious, I would have seen myself, in New York City, about to be sacrificed by Ciaran's coven for my own powers.

No thank you. No more of this. The Goddess must have thought I was ready for this, but I didn't *feel* ready.

Once again I gazed at my red candle. My situation was strange: I was an unusually powerful blood witch. Yet because Wicca had discovered me only about three months ago, I was relatively unschooled in magick. Even as hard as I had been trying to learn, the breadth and depth of a witch's knowledge ensured that I would be at it my whole life. Another fact was that I was uninitiated. An uninitiated witch was not in command of her full powers—in fact, not exactly in command of her powers at all. Which was what everyone kept trying to tell me.

Until now I had loved feeling my powers stretch and grow, like a plant toward sunlight. The more I made magick, the stronger my magick seemed and the easier it was to make it flow. I had believed that my magick would be good, that I would walk in sunlight even though I was Woodbane. Belwicket had been a Woodbane coven but had renounced dark magick centuries ago. But then I had found out Ciaran was my father, and all of my assumptions had snapped. I was no longer sure that I would use magick for goodness. No longer sure that I could stay out of the shadows. Now with every breath I remembered that I had been born of evil, the daughter of a murderer. And that it had cost me Hunter.

I have a choice, I thought. I choose to work good magick.

I looked at my altar and concentrated, centering myself and focusing my energy. Rise, I thought, looking at the silver bowl holding the incense. "Rise, be light, be light as air. I lift you up and hold you there." The little rhyme came into my head, and simultaneously the silver bowl wobbled a bit, then shakily rose above my altar. It hovered there, weightless, while I stared at it in shock. Oh God, I thought. Wicca had shown me many things in the last three months that I never would have thought possible, but the idea that I had the power to levitate anything amazed me.

Okay, concentrate, I told myself as the bowl tilted. I concentrated. Almost immediately it steadied.

Next I made the candle rise and kept the two objects floating before me. Could I make it three? Yes. The bowl of water rose gracefully. I was able to keep them steadier now, and the three objects bobbed before me as I turned my attention to the bowl of crystals. This was amazing, intense magick. I could tell none of this skill came from my friend Alyce Fernbrake, who had shared all of her knowledge with me in a powerful ritual called tàth meànma brach.

This was mine; this power was me. It was beautiful and good in a way I could never be.

A slight vibration in the floor barely registered with me as I began to levitate the bowl of crystals in the air. More thin, light, striations of sound—distracting me . . . Crap, they were footsteps!

I leaped up, shoved the altar behind my desk, and kicked the silver bowls and candle out of the way. Hoping I hadn't burned the rug, I jumped into bed. I was pulling the covers up when the door to my room opened.

"Morgan?" my mom whispered, peering into my room.

Asleep, I'm asleep, I thought, feeling my eyelids get heavy. My mother gently closed the door, and I heard her walk down the hallway. I waited until I heard the door to her own room close, then I slunk out of bed and tried to clean up soundlessly. This had been so stupid. I had been so full of myself that I hadn't remembered to put up a border spell that would alert me when my parents came home. I hadn't been casting my senses, paying attention to my surroundings.

Gently I shoved my altar back into my closet. I took off the robe and gathered the bowls and tools and hid them with the altar. Tomorrow I would put them where I usually hid them: behind the HVAC vent in the hallway. Pretty full of yourself, aren't you? I thought with disgust as I tried to scrape up the sand with my hands. You just want to make any kind of magick you can, with no thought as to the consequences. That's a Woodbane way to behave.

I cleaned up the circle as best I could, knowing I would have to finish tomorrow. I brushed my teeth and got into my pj's. Then I climbed back into bed and pulled up the covers. All of my misery was back and more. I had missed a coven circle tonight. I was Ciaran's daughter. I didn't have Hunter. If things were this bad when I was only seventeen, what would they be like when I hit thirty?

2. Alone

Brother Colin, I shall not prevaricate to you, who are my flesh and blood as well as a fellow servant of God. I have only begun my work here and shall be content if it takes me until the end of my days to reach the people of Barra Head. But it has been a surprise to discover how the populace resists the Good Word. There is a handful of devout souls, to be sure, but everywhere the old religion pervades. Where I look, I see ancient sigils chipped into rock faces, painted on the crude sod and stone houses: even herb gardens grown in heathen patterns. Surely God has sent me here to save these people, these so called Wodebaynes.

—Brother Sinestus Tor, to his brother Colin, November 1767

Hours later I lay in bed, watching the interplay of shadows on my recently painted bedroom walls. I'd thought I was exhausted, but sleep hadn't come. Now I let my senses float out into the house. Mary K., separated from me by a bathroom, was deeply asleep. She'd come home shortly after my parents had, completely excited by the prospect of eleven days at her friend

Jaycee's house: an uninterrupted slumber party. Her three suitcases were already packed and by the front door.

My parents, too, were asleep: my mother lightly, fitfully, my dad more deeply. They were nervous about the trip, about being away from us.

I turned on my side. Tonight I'd made objects levitate. It had been amazing and even a little frightening. If I weren't so distraught, it would have been joyful, beautiful. Well, that was Wicca: light and dark at the same time and part of the same thing. Day turning into night. Beauty and ugliness, good and bad. The rose and the thorn.

Morgan. As the voice echoed inside my head, I blinked, sending my senses out more strongly. Oh my God, Hunter was right outside the front door. It was one-thirty in the morning. I had two thoughts: I can't face him. And: I hope he doesn't wake my parents.

Morgan. I bit my lip and got of bed, knowing I had no choice. Despite my unhappiness, my traitorous heart skipped a beat in anticipation of seeing Hunter. Very quietly I pushed my feet into my bear claw slippers and padded downstairs. I put on my parka and opened the front door as silently as I could.

He stood there, his fine, fair hair glinting with winter moonlight. His face was in darkness, but I saw the hard line of his jaw, the sculpted curve of his cheekbone. It had been only a few days, but I longed for him with a physical ache.

"Hi," I said, looking away from him. My hair was unbrushed, and my face felt tired and drawn.

"You missed a circle," he said evenly, tilting his head back to see me. The cold January air made his words come out like a dragon's breath. "Why?"

Experienced witches can lie and deceive each other fairly successfully. But if I lied to Hunter, he would know it. "I didn't want to see you." I tried to sound strong, but I'm sure my body language was screaming anguish.

"Why?" His expression didn't change, but I could sense the hurt and anger I had caused him. "Am I *repellent* now?"

I shook my head. "Of course not," I said. "But I wanted more time alone since we just broke up."

"Part of Wicca is making the commitment to observe the turning of the Wheel," Hunter said. "The weekly circle is just as important as your personal life."

Count to ten before you speak, I reminded myself. He made it sound like I had missed the circle because I had a *zit*. But he had seen how upset and shocked and freaked out I had been after what had happened in New York—after finding out that my father wasn't gentle Angus Bramson, the man who had loved and lived with my mother for several years, but Ciaran MacEwan, the evil and destructive witch who had eventually killed her. Hunter had seen for himself how ruthless Ciaran was, so much a pure Woodbane, dedicated to acquiring power at any cost. With a father like that, did I have a chance of turning out okay? I was pure Woodbane myself. Was it just a matter of time before I was lured by dark magick? And how could I stand to see the look on Hunter's face if and when I finally went bad? His horror and disillusionment?

"I know the circle is important," I said stiffly. "But I wanted some time alone."

"I guess it's a matter of priorities," he said in a tone he knew infuriated me.

Knowing that he was trying to goad me didn't stop me from

reacting as if he had thrown a match onto a puddle of gasoline.

"My priorities are to keep you and everyone else in Kithic away from a potentially evil influence!" I hissed into the night air.

"Funny how you can decide what's best for us all." Hunter, of all people, knew exactly how to get to me. "You'd do well to remember just how little training you have. Perhaps we can make our own decisions about who we want to associate with. Who we want to make magick with."

I looked at Hunter, trying to control my anger. I knew that he was angry with me for missing the circle, but it was infuriating that he could ignore what had happened between us so easily—that my being a powerful witch meant I wasn't allowed to have human emotions. I had spent the last few days in complete misery; how could I just go back to the circles like nothing had happened to me?

"Plus there's the fact that I don't love you," I said finally, praying for this conversation to end. "That had something to do with it."

Hunter's green eyes were shaded gray by the pale light. But they seemed to look right through my eyes into my psyche, into the innermost me. He knew I was lying.

"We should be together." His words sounded like they cost him.

"We *can't*." My throat felt thick.

He looked up at the heavy white clouds scudding across the night sky. "You should come to circles. If not with Kithic, then with another coven."

My heart hurt. I wanted so much to tell him about my levitating experience. But it was better for him if I didn't. If I didn't share myself with him at all. Suddenly exhausted, I turned to the front door.

"Good night, Hunter."

"So you say."

His voice rang in my ears as I slipped into the house.

"Morning!" Mary K. sang, unnaturally perky as usual. All of the Rowlandses were morning people, wide awake with the sunrise and ready to go long before my natural biorhythms had kicked me into a vertical position. Before Mary K. and I knew I was adopted, it had been a family joke that I stood out so much. No one mentioned it anymore.

"Morning, honey," my mom said briefly, then turned to me. "Morgan, Dad and I are still concerned about you staying in the house alone. But I understand that if you stayed at Eileen and Paula's, you would have a longer commute to and from school."

"Much longer," I said. "Like forty-five minutes."

"Not that it would kill you to get up earlier," Mom went on. "But your father and I have discussed it, and we trust you to stay here because we know that you would *never* want to let us down or make us feel that trust was misplaced."

"Uh-huh," I said. Behind Mom, Mary K. watched us with interest.

"But to be on the safe side," Mom went on, "I've jotted down a few house rules. I'd like you to read them and make sure you understand everything."

My eyes went wide as she handed me a sheet of notepaper. I took it from her and slowly read it while Mary K. hovered, barely disguising her curiosity.

It was about the behavior they expected me to display while they were out of town. Display? I thought. As if I would be doing everything out on the front lawn. I read further. It basically said no boys in the house, I couldn't miss school, I had to do my homework, call Aunt Eileen every day and check in, I couldn't have parties. . . .

My response was crucial here—I was awake enough to recognize that.

"Well, it looks like you covered everything," I began.

My dad came in then and headed for the coffeemaker. He glanced over at us and made the strategic decision to take his coffee into the living room.

"I mean, it seems fair," I told her. "Pretty much common sense."

"So all this seems okay?" Mom asked.

"Well, sure," I said. "I mean, I wouldn't be having parties, anyway."

"Or boys in the house? Hunter?"

I tried not to wince. "We broke up, remember?"

"Oh, honey, I'm sorry for mentioning it," Mom said, looking concerned. "Will you be all right alone?"

"Of course I will, Mom. I'm fine."

She hesitated, but I waved her off, plastering a cheerful smile on my face. After Mom went upstairs, I sat with my tea while Mary K. perched on a chair across from me, her big brown eyes asking for details. "What were all those rules about?"

"Oh, about being straight and narrow while they were gone, like a saint."

"Really? So no orgies?"

I groaned. "So funny."

She giggled. "I can't believe they gave you a list of rules. It's not like you're Bree."

Bree Warren had been my best friend for eleven years, until Cal Blaire had moved to Widow's Vale. When she first laid eyes on Cal, she knew that she wanted him, but he wanted me, and Bree did not take it well. The story got more complicated from there. She and Cal slept together before Cal became my boyfriend, and Cal tried to kill me when I refused to practice dark magick with his mother's coven. It had all come to a close one horrible night in his mother's library, when both Cal and his mother, Selene, were killed as she tried to steal my powers. Bree and I had been trying to forge a new friendship, but we were moving slowly.

Mary K. was referring to the fact that Bree's parents were divorced, and she lived with her dad. Mr. Warren was a lawyer with tons of money and not much time for Bree. She often stayed by herself in their big house for weeks at a time, which gave her a lot of opportunity to experiment. Bree wasn't really wild, but she was rich and unsupervised.

"No, I'm not Bree," I agreed.

"Are you going to follow the rules or blow them off?"

My sister's sweet expression and innocent demeanor always made me forget that she was very shrewd for a fourteen-year-old.

"Ugh." I put my head down on the table. "They make me feel like I'm ten years old."

Mary K. giggled and put down her mug. "It'll be good for you, Saint Morgan," she said, standing up. "Like penance."

"Good-bye, honey," my mom said an hour later. "Be careful. And if you need anything, call Eileen."

"Sure," I said. "Don't worry."

"I *will* worry," she said, looking into my eyes. "That's what mothers do."

All at once I got that awful feeling in my throat that signaled I was about to cry. I reached over and hugged the only mother I had ever known, and she hugged me back.

"I love you," I said, feeling embarrassed and sad. I realized I would miss them while they were away.

"I love you, too, honey." Then she turned and got into Dad's car, and Mary K. waved at me from the backseat. I waved back and watched the car until it went around the corner and I couldn't see it anymore. Then I realized I was freezing, standing out here, and went into the house that would be mine alone for the next eleven days.

It was extremely quiet inside. Casting my senses, I picked up only Dagda, sleeping deeply as usual. The refrigerator hummed in the kitchen; the grandfather clock my dad had built from a kit ticked loudly. With irrational panic, I suddenly felt like every ax murderer in the area was pricking up his ears, knowing he should home in on this address right away.

"Stop it," I told myself in disgust, plopping down in front of the TV.

When the doorbell rang half an hour later, I jumped a foot in the air. I hadn't perceived anyone coming up the walk, and that realization made my heart kick into overdrive.

I cast my senses strongly as I crept over to peer through the peephole. I sensed a blood witch right before I saw the small, red-haired woman on the front porch. A witch, but no one I knew. I didn't feel any danger, but I might not, if she was powerful enough.

I opened the door. A strong witch who wanted to come into the house could probably do it despite the ward-evil and boundary spells I had set all around the house.

"Hello, Morgan," she said. Her eyes were a light, warm brown, like caramel. "My name is Eoife McNabb. I'm a subelder of the council. I want to talk to you about Ciaran MacEwan. Your father."

3. Challenge

Winter has set upon us, Brother Colin, and it is a raw one, compared to Weymouth's mildness. It does not freeze, nor yet snow, but it is cold with a wetness that chills one's bones to the marrow. Brother Colin, I have not wavered in my devotion to these people and my blessed calling of spreading God's Word. But I tell you, the people of Barra Head have a deep suspicion of me, the other brothers (we are five), and even our blessed Father Benedict, who is as holy a man as I have known. Heads turn away as we walk through the village, dogs bark, children run and hide. Today I found a marking drawn on the abbey door. It was a star encircled. The sight of this devil's mark made my blood run cold.

—Brother Sinestus Tor, to Colin, January 1768

I stood in my doorway a moment, blinking stupidly at Eoife McNabb. I felt like she'd just somehow sucked all the air out of my lungs.

At last I realized I was being rude. "Um—do you want to come in?" I asked.

"Yes, thank you." She stepped in and looked around our hallway and living room with interest. From what I could pick up, she was worried, a little tense, and unsure about coming here. I guess she felt me scanning her senses because she blinked and looked at me more closely.

"Um, sit down, Eva," I said, waving a hand at the couch. "Do you want something to drink? Some tea?" Since she had (I thought) a Scottish accent, I figured tea was a safe bet.

"It's Eoife," she corrected me. "*E-o-i-f-e*. Tea would be lovely, thanks."

"Eef-uh?"

She gave a slight smile. "Close enough." She stepped into the living room and took off her heavy wool coat. Underneath she was dressed in black pants and a pink turtleneck that clashed amazingly with her carrot-colored hair. Her image stayed with me as I went into the kitchen to put the kettle on. She had no freckles to go with that hair. Her face was smooth and unlined, but she gave the impression of being older than she looked. In her forties, maybe? It was impossible to tell.

I brought the tray out a few minutes later. Eoife waited until we had our cups in front of us, and then she looked at me, as if I were an exhibit she'd heard a lot about and was finally seeing. I looked back at her.

"How do you know me?" I asked.

She took a sip of her tea. "There are very few council members who don't know about you," she said. "Of course we'd been watching Selene Belltower for years, and anyone who came into contact with her. From the very beginning, the council has found you extremely interesting. Then recently we learned that you were the daughter of Ciaran MacEwan and Maeve

Riordan. As you can imagine, that heightened our interest."

I could feel my eyes widening. "You mean the council has been spying on me?"

For a moment Eoife looked almost uncomfortable, but the expression passed so quickly that I wasn't sure if I had imagined it or not.

"No, not spying," she said, in her melodic Scottish accent. "But surely you of all people understand that there are dark forces out there. The council tries to protect *all* witches: especially those who practice only bright magick, who understand the dangers of the dark."

Then where were you when I was in danger of having my power sucked out in New York? I thought angrily.

"We know, of course, what happened to you in New York," Eoife said, and I wondered if she was aware of my thoughts. It was incredibly irritating. "It was appalling," she went on quietly. "It must have been horrific for you. Someday the council would like to hear the whole story—not just what Hunter knows."

A cold fist gripped my heart. Hunter. Of course. He was a Seeker for the council. What had he told them? He knew more about me than anyone else. I felt sick.

I took a sip of tea, trying to calm down. It didn't have the life-affirming jolt that Diet Coke had, but I was getting used to it. It was a very witchy drink.

"Okay, so Hunter's been reporting on me." I tried to sound casual. "Fine. But why, exactly, are you so interested in me now?" Three months ago I would have been too insecure and intimidated to be this direct. Almost being killed more than once had put insecurity into perspective.

"Hunter is your loyal friend," Eoife said. "And we're interested in you for several reasons. First, because you've impressed several of our contacts with your remarkable power. Some of the things you're apparently capable of are simply unfathomable, coming from an uninitiated witch who's been studying only three months. Second, because you're the daughter of two extremely powerful witches—a daughter we didn't know either of them had. Bradhadair was the strongest witch Belwicket had seen in generations."

Bradhadair had been Maeve's coven name. It meant "Fire Fairy."

"We know about Ciaran's other children, of course," Eoife went on. "To tell you the truth, none of them has caused waves of excitement."

Ciaran had three children with his estranged wife, back in Scotland. I had met one of them, Killian, in New York. My half brother. Ciaran and Maeve had been lovers, and I was the illegitimate result. Ciaran hadn't even known I existed until a few days ago.

"The council needs you to find Ciaran."

Eoife dropped this bomb right after I had taken a sip of tea, and I almost spit it out all over her. I gulped and swallowed, trying not to cough.

"What?" I asked.

"Do you know what a dark wave is?" Eoife asked.

"It's . . . devastation," I said. "I read about it in my mother's Book of Shadows. A dark wave can kill people, level houses, destroy whole villages, whole covens."

"You have Maeve of Belwicket's Book of Shadows?" Eoife's eyes practically gleamed.

"Yes," I said quietly, feeling a little resentful of her excitement. "But it's private."

She sat back and looked at me. "You're very . . . interesting," she said, as if speaking to herself. "Very interesting." Then she remembered where we were in the conversation. "Yes. In essence, a dark wave is destruction. Utter destruction. Belwicket was obliterated by one. Until recently, no one knew Maeve and Angus had survived."

Angus Bramson had been Maeve's lover also. They had known each other since childhood and had lived together after they had fled to America. But Angus wasn't her mùirn beatha dàn. Maeve loved him, but she never felt the connection to him that she did to Ciaran. Maeve had never married Angus, and he wasn't my father. But he had died by Maeve's side in a barn in upstate New York. Ciaran had locked them in the barn and set it on fire.

"Belwicket isn't the only coven that has been decimated by a dark wave," Eoife went on. She took a picture out of her black leather briefcase. "This was Riverwarry," she said, handing me the photograph. It was a black-and-white shot of a charming village. I couldn't tell if it was Irish, English, Scottish, or Welsh.

"This is Riverwarry now," she went on, handing me another photograph.

My heart filled with sadness as I saw what had happened to Riverwarry. It looked like a bomb had gone off right in the center of the village. Only rubble remained: bits of wall, shiny, melted lumps of glass that had once been windows, blackened remains of trees and shrubs. I was afraid to look too closely—in Maeve's BOS, she had described how she had seen the body of her cat among the ruins and her mother's hand beneath a crumpled wall.

"There are many others," Eoife said, gesturing to a stack of photographs in her briefcase. "Chip Munding, Betts' Field, the MacDougals, Knifewind, Crossbrig, Hollysberry, Incdunning. Among others."

"Why were these covens destroyed?"

"Because they had knowledge and power," Eoife said simply. "They had books, spells, tools, charts, or maps that Amyranth wanted. Amyranth gathers knowledge at any price. As you know, they are willing to steal power from witches outside their coven to make themselves stronger. We call them old Woodbanes because they conform more closely to the traditional Woodbane tenets: knowledge is power, and power above all."

Of course she knew I was Woodbane. Belwicket had been a coven of "new" Woodbanes, those who had renounced dark magick and sworn to make only good and positive magick. Ciaran was one of the old Woodbanes. Yet he and Maeve had slept together and made me, a Woodbane who had one foot in darkness and one foot in light.

"These pictures are awful. But what do they have to do with me?" I asked.

"We've recently received information that Amyranth is planning on calling another dark wave," Eoife said. She tucked the photographs back into her briefcase. "Here, in Widow's Vale. They plan to wipe out the Starlocket coven."

My mouth dropped open. Whatever I had expected, it wasn't this. Starlocket had once been Selene Belltower's coven. When Selene had fled Widow's Vale, her most loyal Woodbane followers had disappeared with her. But not all of Starlocket had been Woodbane or dark Woodbanes. The members that had been from the other great clans—Leapvaughn, Brightendale, Vikroth, Rowanwand, Burnhide, or Wyndenkell—and also those who were not blood witches had continued on under the leadership of my friend Alyce Fernbrake. Alyce owned Practical Magick, a store in the next town over that specialized in Wiccan necessities. Ever since I first discovered my powers, Alyce had been a kind adviser, and after our tàth meànma brach, in which we shared one another's knowledge and experiences, I felt a special closeness to her.

Now my birth father and his coven were planning to plunder Starlocket for its books, tools, spells, star charts—anything they could find. Not only that. I knew from bitter firsthand experience that Amyranth could actually steal people's magick, their power and their knowledge, in a dark ritual. Unfortunately, the person didn't usually live through it. That was what had almost happened to me in New York before Ciaran had helped Hunter stop the ritual.

"How do you know about this?" I asked faintly.

"We had an agent who infiltrated the San Francisco cell of Amyranth. It was in the last message she sent us," Eoife said. "Right before she died."

I was startled. "Died?"

"She was killed," said Eoife sadly. "Found drowned in the bay, with the Amyranth sigil burned into her skin."

"Oh, Goddess." My brain began piecing together ideas. "But if she was killed because of passing on that message, then surely Amyranth knows the council is onto them. Surely they'll change their plans," I said.

"We thought of that. But it's not necessarily true. After all," Eoife went on, her voice turning bitter, "we've been singularly ineffectual in finding out anything about most cells of Amyranth—especially the New York one. And even having this bit of information doesn't really help us. Alyce and some of the other Starlocket members have been having disturbing visions. Some of their spells have gone terribly awry. They have bad dreams. It all feels like a noose closing around their necks."

"But why can't the council help? Isn't it made up of some of the strongest witches alive?"

Eoife looked at me with anger. "Yes. But we're not gods or goddesses. Simply knowing about a dark wave doesn't help us stop it. Frankly, we have no idea how to stop it."

"So what can I do?" I asked carefully.

My guest took a deep breath, trying to control her emotions. Her fingers trembled almost imperceptibly as she sipped tea that by now must be cold.

"We want you to help us stop the dark wave," she said.

My world went white in an instant. Jagged images of what had almost happened to me in New York crashed into my mind, and my breath went shallow. With tunnel vision I stared at Eoife, sure that horror and panic were written on my face.

"Eoife," I breathed. "I'm seventeen years old. I'm not initiated. I don't see how I can help with *anything*."

"We know about your situation. But you have a great deal of power." She tried to keep defeat out of her voice but didn't succeed. "And you're our only hope."

"Why?"

She looked at me. "You're Ciaran's daughter. His daughter by the woman he loved. And you're very, very powerful. He would be intensely attracted to that. You could get close to him."

"And *then* what?" I was trying not to sound hysterical. Inside my thoughts were running around like a chicken with its head cut off.

"We need information," Eoife said. "We have strong evidence that Amyranth is planning a strike on Starlocket during its Imbolc celebration. There's a possibility we *could* stop them if you could learn something—anything—of the spell they plan to use to call the dark wave. Knowing even a few of these words would help us fight it. If Ciaran were to make you his confidante, you might be able to get us this information."

I looked at Eoife in disbelief. "And what if he tries to *kill* me?"

"He's your father," she said. "He didn't let his coven kill you in New York."

I crossed my arms over my chest and sighed. "Okay. Get close to Ciaran. Discover what I can of the dark-wave spell. God, this is so surreal."

Eoife gave me a level glance. "There's more."

"Why am I not surprised?" I muttered.

Eoife shifted in her chair. "If you planted a watch sigil on him, it would help us track his movements. We'd have a better chance of knowing where he was."

"How am I supposed to plant a watch sigil on him? He's a thousand times stronger than me!" I was frightened now and running out of patience with this crazy conversation. What this woman was suggesting could easily get me killed.

"We don't believe he's a thousand times stronger than you," Eoife said, but her gaze dropped from mine. "Anyway, we would teach you how to do it. We would cover you with deception spells, with protection, with every weapon we have. With luck, you could even attend an Amyranth circle. Any information you pick up there would be useful. The more we know about them, the more chance we have of being able to dismantle their coven, remove their power, scatter them so they could never again call on a dark wave to obliterate a clan, to pillage their knowledge, to destroy their homes. With your help, we can save Starlocket. Without your help, they are surely lost."

"The witches in Amyranth would recognize me," I pointed out.

"But now they know you're Ciaran's daughter," Eoife said. "They would believe you'd want to be close to him."

This was all just too incredible, too absurd. "You *must* have someone more qualified," I said.

"We don't, Morgan," Eoife said. "The San Francisco cell of Amyranth is the only one we've been able to infiltrate—and that was unsuccessful. It's only because we're so desperate, so without options, that we even considered asking you to take this risk. Amyranth has been gaining power for the last thirty years, and we've made hardly any progress in fighting them. But now we have you, the daughter of one of the main leaders. Ciaran is incredibly powerful, incredibly charismatic. Anyone would believe you would want to be closer to him."

"What about you?" I asked. "I'm Ciaran's daughter, after all. Do *you* believe I'd want to be closer to him? Do *you* believe I might actually turn to the darkness?"

The older witch gazed at me steadily. "It's true that great witches have fallen before this. But many have resisted, too, Morgan."

But which will I be? I thought desperately. "Oh, God," I said, standing up and lifting my hair off my neck. I walked around the living room, stretching, not really seeing anything. I realized it was chilly and knelt before the fireplace to make a small tepee of kindling. I looked around for matches, but didn't see any. I thought, *Fire*, and a tiny spark of flame leapt into existence, catching the dry sticks of fatwood, chewing them eagerly. When the kindling was well on its way, I added two small logs, then stood up and brushed off my hands.

"I didn't believe them when they said you could kindle fire," Eoife said. Once again her gaze fixed on me, measuring me, examining me.

I shrugged self-consciously. "I like fire."

"One of my teachers studied with *her* teacher for more than three years to learn how to kindle fire," Eoife said.

Startled, I glanced at her. "How can you even teach it? It's just there."

"No, my dear," she said, softening for the first time since she'd come in. "It isn't. Not usually."

I sat down again and twisted my fingers together. Get close to Ciaran. The idea made my stomach clench. He was my blood father, and he was the epitome of evil, guilty of hundreds of horrible crimes: unaccountable devastation. He was the very image of everything bad that Woodbanes had ever been accused of. He had killed my mother and tried to kill me. Yet . . .

Yet, before I had known who he was, I had felt a strange connection to him, a sort of bond or kinship. I could tell he was very powerful, and I wanted him to teach me what he knew. Then so many things had happened, and I was still sorting out the pieces. Now Eoife wanted me to pretend to have a relationship with him in order to give the council information. Information that would lead to his being stripped of his powers, certainly. I'd watched Hunter perform the spells that wrested a witch's magick from him, and I still shuddered at the memory. I had heard that most witches who had their magick taken away never really recovered. They lived a kind of half life—more of a pale gray existence than a real life. Eoife and the council wanted to do that to Ciaran, and they wanted me to help them.

"I won't lie to you," Eoife said. "This will be very hard, perhaps impossible, and very dangerous. You'll be tempted by darkness, as we all are at times. How well you resist it is up to you. You probably know what is likely to happen to you if you are found out, if you fail." She looked down at her hands in her lap. "But if you succeed—you will have saved not only Starlocket, but all the covens and clans after them, the ones who will in the future be targeted for a dark wave. And . . . you would have more power."

I looked at Eoife. "Magickal power?"

"Perhaps, though that isn't what I meant. I meant the power that comes from doing something profoundly good and selfless, the power that comes from putting good out into the world. Remember, what you send out is thrice returned."

"Does Hunter know about this? What you're asking?"

"Yes. He's against it. But this decision is yours."

"What makes you so sure Ciaran will trust me?" I asked.

"We're not," Eoife admitted. "But you're our only hope."

I paced the room. I noticed it was dark outside—hours had passed since Eoife had come. My parents might be boarding their cruise ship by now.

What if I failed? Not only would Alyce and the rest of Starlocket die, but I would be forever corrupted. If I wasn't strong enough to resist Ciaran, I would become as evil as he was. On the other hand, where was I now? I had lost Hunter, I was afraid to make magick with my coven. . . . What did I have left to lose? How strong was I? Think, think.

Eoife waited patiently, just as her teacher who was trying to kindle fire must have waited patiently for three years, trying to learn it. I wasn't patient. I didn't have the inner calm that most witches had, the inner compass that allowed them to stay on track, stay focused yet completely connected with the world. I didn't know if I would ever have it.

Could I do good?

Oh, Goddess, help me.

I don't know how much time passed. Finally I turned to look at Eoife, so small and still, like a garden statue.

"I'll do it," I said.

4. Danger

Brother Colin, my hand shakes as I write this. I have told all to Father Benedict, and he is praying on the matter now. Tonight after matins I found I could not sleep and determined to walk in the chill air along the cliffs in the hopes that healthy exercise would help me to rest.

I set out at a brisk pace, giving thanks for my sturdy wool cloak. After a time I spied the glow of a cheerful fire. Thinking it was a lone shepherd, I hastened to join him and share in the warmth before heading back to the abbey. Coming quite close, I saw this was no lone shepherd, but a group of people. Women from Barra Head, each soul bare to the sky, danced in pagan nudity around the fire, wailing some unearthly song.

Horror overwhelmed me, and after but a few moments I dashed away from the evil place. I immediately found Father Benedict and confessed what I had seen. What do you make of this, Brother Colin? I had assumed that Wodebayne was simply a clan name, but now I wonder if they are some darker, heathen sect. Please send me your earliest counsel, for I am most distraught.

—Brother Sinestus Tor, March 1768

To my surprise, Eoife McNabb didn't jump up and down in joy at my announcement. She looked very solemn and then nodded slowly. "I was hoping you would say that."

I released a deep breath and tried to relax. "So what now?"

"Well, you'll need to go to New York at once," she said.

"What? I can't." I shook my head. "My folks are out of town, and I have to house-sit and cat-sit and go to school every day, or they'll kill me."

Eoife blinked once, and we looked at each other. Realizing the ridiculousness of my situation, I began to laugh nervously. After a moment of surprise, Eoife smiled.

"All right," she said, shrugging. "I know that you're unusually young to have so much power. But remember, we're talking about the destruction of countless innocent witches. There has to be a way for you to help us and still keep your grades up and feed your cat."

As if he'd been called, Dagda prowled into the room and fixed his green eyes on Eoife. He walked toward her, sniffed her delicately, then presented his triangular head for petting.

"You're a beauty," Eoife murmured while he purred. Finally he purred so hard, he fell over on his side, and she tickled his gray tummy.

"You must stay in Widow's Vale," she said, thinking aloud.

"Yeah."

"Right. Let's see. You met your half brother Killian in New York, yes?"

"Yes." I nodded.

"Does he know you're his sister?"

"I don't think so. By the time I found out, he had disappeared. I haven't seen him since then."

"We're speculating that he was supposed to take part in Amyranth's ritual," Eoife explained. "Ciaran would like one, any one, of his children to be a worthy successor. If that was Killian's test but he left town instead, Ciaran would be furious with him."

"He didn't strike me as a coven leader," I said. "He seemed more like just a party guy to me."

"Killian isn't power hungry, like Ciaran," Eoife said. "But he does seem to be amoral—he does what he wants but for the pleasure of it, not to gain anything. I'm thinking—maybe the way to get to Ciaran is through Killian. We could get Killian to come here somehow. He'd come out of curiosity, if nothing else. Once Killian is here, explain your relationship to him. Then ask him to have Ciaran come here so you can get to know him better, as his daughter."

A chill went down my spine, despite the cheerful warmth of the fire. It was horrible—the name Ciaran brought such conflicting images and feelings: the understanding, compelling man at the bookstore and then the terrifying, powerful Woodbane witch who had wanted to take my magick by force. He terrified me in a way that nothing else did, and . . . he was my father. I wanted to know him. And how would I hold out for one second against his power if he really wanted me to join him in Amyranth? I would have no chance.

"You have until Imbolc," she said, interrupting my thoughts.

Imbolc was February 2. Less than two weeks. Two weeks

from now, what would I be? Alive? Dead? Evil? I felt like throwing up.

"A few more things," Eoife said, sounding businesslike. She poured herself more hot water from the teapot and once again steeped the tea leaves. Their smooth, complex, smoky fragrance rose through the air. "One, you'll be functioning as a council agent and as such will check in with your council mentor, who is me. We can set up a contact schedule. If I'm not available, Hunter will take your reports."

Great, I thought, already feeling the pain that seeing him would bring. Somehow I didn't think that Eoife would care that we were broken up.

"Second, we'll be teaching you the spells you need to help you through this. It goes without saying that learning them perfectly is imperative."

No kidding, I thought. Crap. What had I gotten myself into?

Her face softened, and I wondered again if she was in tune with my thoughts. "This could be worse than what happened in New York, but I wouldn't ask you to do it if I thought the mission was hopeless. I—and the rest of the council—truly feel that you can do this."

I digested this. "Okay. So now I call Killian?"

"Do you have his phone number?" She looked surprised.

"No," I said, confused. "I thought you meant, you know, a witch message."

Her face was carefully blank. "You can send messages? With your mind?"

Why didn't I just get "Zoo Exhibit" tattooed on my forehead? "Uh-huh."

Eoife swallowed. "I thought Hunter was exaggerating," she

said quietly. "An uninitiated witch—kindling fire. Sending witch messages. Calling on the ancient lines of power. Even putting a holding spell on Hunter. I couldn't believe it was true, though Hunter has never been inaccurate before. I came here expecting to leave in disappointment. Expecting to go back to the council and tell them we had no hope."

"Then why did you even go through this?" I asked. "Telling me you'd teach me the spells, that you'd help me. That I was your only hope. Why do it if you really thought I wouldn't be able to help you?"

"I was doing as I was instructed," she replied with dignity. "Believe me, I far prefer this reality to what I was afraid I would find. Now I think it's time to call Killian."

"Okay," I said. Killian, I thought, sending it toward him. Killian. Come to Widow's Vale. For long minutes we sat silently. I wondered how far away Killian was and if that made any difference. But then I felt his response.

I took a minute to breathe and orient myself. When I stood, I felt creaky, like I had been there for hours. "Okay," I told Eoife. "I think he's going to come."

"Very good," said Eoife. "Morgan, I'm going to teach you the watch sigil in case things start to move quickly and you have the opportunity to mark Ciaran before we meet again."

I nodded and watched Eoife carefully as she drew the sigil in the air.

"The symbol itself is not complicated," she continued. "What will be difficult is getting close enough to Ciaran to place it on him without his detection. Practice the sigil so that you'll be ready when the opportunity presents itself."

Slowly I began to mirror Eoife's motions in the air. "All

right," I said finally. "I think I've got it. I'll keep practicing when you leave."

Eoife nodded. "Excellent." She reached for her briefcase and stood, glancing around to make sure she hadn't forgotten anything. "I'm glad to have met you, Morgan Riordan," she said formally, holding out her hand to shake.

"Rowlands," I said, frowning. "That's my last name."

Her eyebrows drew together. "Oh, of course. I'm going to report back to the council about the nature of our plan and that you've sent Killian a message. I'll check in with you soon to set up a time for you to start learning spells."

"Okay." I walked her to the front door, feeling a deep sense of foreboding. After what happened in New York, I had hoped to lie low for a while, to have everything be calm and quiet. Now I was signed up to enter the lion's den. And I might not make it out alive.

"You know you're more than welcome to come stay," said Aunt Eileen an hour later.

I had called her to check in, though my parents hadn't been gone even a whole day yet. I had needed some normalcy after the surreal visit with Eoife McNabb. "Oh, no, I'll be fine," I said. "I'm just going to go to school, do homework, eat, and sleep." Oh, and try to trap one of the world's most dangerous Woodbanes. That, too.

"Okay," she said. "But promise you'll call us anytime, day or night, if you need anything or want to talk or feel worried. All right?"

"Okeydokey," I said, trying to sound cheerful.

As soon as I hung up, I felt my senses start to tingle. I opened the front door and saw Hunter at the end of our dark walkway, heading for the house. He looked up, saw me, and didn't smile.

Just seeing him made me want to cry. This was the one person who could comfort me, who would understand, who would be on my side. Yet I couldn't be with him, couldn't turn to him for support or love. I knew that it was better to hurt him now than crush him later—what if I turned on him down the road? After seeing what Ciaran had been willing to do to me, I could only imagine the pain I could cause Hunter if and when my evil Woodbane nature showed itself. As painful as this separation was, surely it was better than the pain of knowing I had attacked him from the darkness.

Typically, he didn't say hello. He just leaned against the house while I rubbed my shoulders to keep warm. It was another bitter night. He waited until I met his eyes, then launched in.

"I can't believe you've decided to go along with this ridiculous, far-fetched plan!" he began, his English accent more pronounced than usual. "Do you have any idea how dangerous it's going to be? Do you have any idea what you're up against? This isn't one of our circles! This is life or death!"

"I know," I said quietly. "I was there in New York, remember?"

"Exactly! So how can you even consider going along with this? It's *not* your responsibility."

I just looked at him. In the dim yellow glare of the front porch light he looked gorgeous, as usual, and angry, which also seemed fairly common these days. But I had also seen him laughing, his head thrown back; I had seen his face flushed with desire; I had seen the look in his eyes before he kissed me. My chest felt fluttery as I thought about it, and I rubbed my arms again, grateful for the distraction of the cold.

"Have you heard anything more about your parents?" I asked. In New York, Hunter had made the decision to begin looking for them. I knew that the loss of his mother and father was a huge event in his life, and it hurt me to see him unable to find them.

Hunter's angry expression softened slightly. He looked away. "No," he said. "Nothing. You're changing the subject. I don't want to talk about it." He looked me in the eye briefly. "These last few days haven't been a lark for me, either, Morgan."

I nodded, unable to speak. God, I hated not being in his life like I had been. I wanted to comfort him, to tell him it would be okay, but now I was the person who was causing part of his pain.

"It's cold," he said unnecessarily. "Why are we out here? Let's go in." He moved toward the door, but I held up my hand.

"No," I said.

"Why?" His perfect brows arched over eyes as green as sea glass. All I wanted was for him to hold me and comfort me and tell me everything was going to be all right.

"Remember, I told you about my folks going on a cruise? They left today."

"Where's Mary K.?"

"Jaycee's."

His face took on a speculative expression, and I braced myself.

"You're saying you're alone in the house," he said.

"Yes."

"That cruise was for . . . eleven days?"

"Yes." I sighed.

"So you're alone in the house. All by yourself."

"Yes." I couldn't look at him—his voice had softened, and the anger was gone. Oh, Goddess, he was so attractive to me. Everything in me responded to everything in him.

"So let's go in." He sounded much calmer than when he had arrived.

I almost whimpered from wanting him. If he came in the house, if we were alone together, how could I keep my hands off him? How could I stop him from putting his hands on me? I wouldn't want to. And what would that do? Making out wouldn't change anything: not my heritage, not my fears, not the possibility that I was going to end up more Ciaran's daughter than Maeve's.

"No, that's not a good idea."

"Got some other guy in there, have you?" His tone was light, but I felt tension coming off him like heat.

"No," I said, looking at my feet. "Look, I just don't want to be alone with you, okay?"

"Then how about my house? We wouldn't be alone there." Hunter lived with his cousin, Sky Eventide.

I gave him my long-suffering look. "I don't think so. We broke up, remember?"

"We should talk about that," he said, frowning. "Speaking of bad ideas."

Tell me about it, I thought. I wanted to be with Hunter more than anything. But I knew—and I had to make myself remember—how terrible it would be to hurt him later. I shook my head to clear it, trying to get back to the subject at hand. "We should *talk* about your trying to control the decisions I make."

Hunter frowned as he seemed to remember why he had

come. "I'm not trying to control your decisions," he said. "I'm trying to help you not make irresponsible ones."

"You think I'm irresponsible?"

"You know I don't. I think you made this decision without having all the facts. Like about exactly how dangerous Ciaran and Amyranth can be. How many deaths they're responsible for. How much power and knowledge they have at their disposal. Pitted against you, a seventeen-year-old uninitiated witch who's been studying Wicca for a grand total of three months."

I knew all that, but hearing him state it so baldly made me cringe. "Yes, I know," I said. "I still think I need to try." I need to know if I'm good or bad, I added to myself. I need to know who my father is, what my heritage is. I need to know that I *can* choose good. If I don't know these things, we can never be together.

"I don't want you to get hurt," he said, his voice sounding frayed. "It's not your job to save the world."

"I'm not trying to save the world," I said. "Just my little part of it. I mean, today it's Starlocket—and Alyce, remember? Tomorrow it's us. Don't you see that?"

Hunter looked around, thinking, deciding on another plan of approach. He was well acquainted with how stubborn I could be, and I could see him weighing his chances of getting through and changing my mind.

He pushed himself off the house and stood before me. "Tell me the instant you hear from Killian," he said.

I tried not to show my surprise. "Okay."

"I don't like this."

"I know."

"I hate this."

"I know."

"Right. So call me."

"I will." After he left, I went back inside, shivering with cold. I sat down in front of the fire and rested my head against the couch. I would have given a lot to have Hunter with me right then. I sighed, wondering if love was always this hard.

5. Connection

I am glad to hear your cough is better, Brother.

As I recounted, the siege (I can only call it thus) has continued against the abbey. Our poor milk cow has gone dry, our kitchen garden has withered, and the mice are keeping our one cat constantly at work. Our daily offices are ever more sparsely attended.

It is the villagers, the Wodebaynes. I know this, though I have not seen it. We are now obliged to buy milk and cheese from a neighbouring farm. Various illnesses have beset us; we cannot shake colds, agues, fevers, etc. It is a desperate time, and I will resort to desperate measures.

—Brother Sinestus, to Colin, May 1768

On Monday morning I saw my sister heading toward our school, followed by some of the Mary K. fan club. I waved at her.

"Mary K.!"

She trotted over, her shiny hair bouncing. I was glad to see her looking more like herself. She'd had a horrible autumn.

Twice I'd stopped her boyfriend, Bakker Blackburn, from practically raping her. After the second time I'd told my parents, who lowered the boom on Mary K. I also told Bakker he'd regret being born if he ever looked at my sister again. I knew we weren't supposed to use magick to harm, but I was absolutely ready to put some serious hurt on Bakker if he hurt Mary K.

But now Mary K. looked happy.

"Hey!" she said.

"Hi," I said, rubbing my eyes. I'd gotten about three hours sleep total. All the little creaks and groans and windows shaking in the wind that I'd never noticed before had been magnified tremendously and made it impossible for me to sleep deeply. "Everything okay?"

"Yep! How about you?"

"Fine. Okay, um, yell if you need anything."

"Sure—thanks." She headed back to the gaggle of freshman friends who were waiting for her. Among them I was surprised to see Alisa Soto, who seemed to be a friend of Jaycee's. Alisa was a sophomore who'd transferred to Widow's Vale High around Christmas, but I had actually hardly seen her at school until today. I knew her because she was in my coven, Kithic—the youngest member. She was one of the people recruited by Bree when Bree had formed a new coven to rival mine and Cal's. When Cal was gone, our two covens had combined to form Kithic, and we were now led by Hunter and Sky.

Most of my coven went to my school: Bree Warren and Robbie Gurevitch, my two best childhood friends, who had recently become a couple; Raven Meltzer, local bad girl and resident goth, who happened to be dating Hunter's cousin, Sky

Eventide; Jenna Ruiz; Matt Adler; Ethan Sharp; and Sharon Goodfine. The last two were a couple, and Jenna and Matt had once been a couple, too, but had broken up.

I was dreading seeing my friends. I didn't know if any of them, aside from Bree and Robbie, knew about me and Hunter. I hadn't wanted to see them Saturday, and I still didn't want to see them. But I had no choice.

All of them, except for Alisa, were sitting, as usual, on the back stairs that led to the school's basement. "Morgan," Robbie greeted me. During our New York trip Robbie had come down on me about my casual misuse of magick. We had made up, but things weren't totally normal yet.

"Hey." My nod included everyone. I popped the top on the Diet Coke I'd bought on my way to school and took a deep slurp. Act casual.

"So how's the bachelorette pad?" Bree asked with a smile.

"Fine. My folks went on a cruise, so I've got the place to myself," I explained to the others. For an instant I thought of Hunter saying, "Let's go in," and my heart contracted.

"Party at Morgan's house," Jenna said, laughing; then her laugh turned into a cough. Bree patted her on the back and looked at me. This cold, damp weather made Jenna's asthma worse.

"No, no party," I said, starting to wake up as the caffeine coursed through my veins. "I can't face the cleanup job after." Plus Mom would have a cow, I thought.

They laughed, and Bree wrapped her arm around Robbie's knee. He looked cautiously pleased. He was crazy about Bree, she seemed to care about him, and they'd been trying to hash out some kind of relationship for a while now. During our trip to New York, they seemed to have made some degree of progress.

"Sky missed you at Saturday's circle," said Sharon. Her black hair swung in a thick curtain just past her shoulders. It was still a little odd to see her all cozy with Ethan, who had been one of the school's biggest potheads until he'd found Wicca. Now he was clean and sober and in love with Sharon.

Raven snorted. "Sky takes everything too seriously." Raven and Sky had been sort of a couple for the last few weeks, but Raven's wandering eye had gotten her into trouble more than once.

Jenna coughed again, and I winced at the sound of her rattly indrawn breath. She looked at me hopefully. I had helped her before, but now I knew that even that kind of magick was forbidden to uninitiated witches. But how could I not help a friend? It seemed so harmless. I hesitated just a minute, then scooted closer to Jenna. She sat up straighter, already anticipating being able to breathe freely again.

I closed my eyes and sank quickly into a deep meditation. I focused on a healing white light and imagined myself grabbing a ribbon of this light out of the air. Then, opening my eyes, I brought my hand to Jenna's back and pressed my palm flat against her thin amethyst sweater. I breathed out, willing the light into Jenna, letting it flow into her lungs, feeling her constricted airways relaxing and opening, all her thirsty cells soaking up oxygen. After just a minute I took my hand away.

"Thanks, Morgan," Jenna said, breathing deeply. "That works so much better than my inhaler."

"You could also wear an amber bead on a silver chain around your neck," Matt surprised us by saying. Seven heads swiveled to look at him. Since he'd cheated on Jenna with Raven, he'd been very quiet and kept a low profile. He always came to circles, always completed the assignments Hunter gave us, but he never participated beyond what was required.

He looked embarrassed by the attention. "I've been doing some reading," he mumbled. "Amber is good for breathing. So's silver."

Jenna looked at him solemnly, at the boy she'd loved for four years until he'd betrayed her. She gave a little nod, and then the morning bell rang. Time to get to class.

I sucked down the last of my Diet Coke and pitched the can into a recycling bin. Our group split up, and Bree and I headed toward our eleventh-grade homeroom. I wished I could tell her about Eoife McNabb and Ciaran and Hunter and everything I was facing. But though I hadn't been officially sworn to secrecy, I knew there was too much at stake to tell anyone who wasn't involved. Not even Bree or Robbie.

"Have you been doing any readings lately?" I asked. Bree had been studying the tarot.

"Uh-huh." Gracefully she swung her black leather backpack onto her other shoulder. Bree was gorgeous. That was the first—and sometimes the only—thing anyone noticed about her. She was taller than me, slender, with a perfect figure. No zit ever dared to mar her skin, her eyes were large, coffee colored, and expressive, and she'd been born with a gift for choosing perfect clothes and makeup. Next to her I usually looked like I ought to have a tool belt strapped to my waist.

"Alyce helped me find another book at Practical Magick that has variant readings of some of the cards. It's so interesting, the whole history of the cards and what they've meant according to what time period they were being read in. It's the first thing in Wicca that I feel I can really relate to."

"That's great," I said. Bree wasn't a blood witch, so while Wicca and magick flowed so naturally to me, it didn't always make it to her. I was glad she'd found something that felt meaningful.

It was hard to go to classes all day, being taught subjects like calc and American history, when I was wondering if my friends were going to be killed by a dark wave soon. It made it difficult to concentrate or to take what the teacher was saying seriously. I tried to keep myself mentally in my classes, but I floated through the day, my mind on other things.

I caught up with Bree on the way to the parking lot after the last bell.

"Your dad out of town again?"

"As usual. I think it's the same woman, in Connecticut. So this makes a record for him—two months with the same person." Since her mother had run off with a younger man when Bree was twelve, Mr. Warren really hadn't had a serious relationship.

"How do you feel about it?" I asked. We pushed through the heavy doors, feeling the force of the cold wind smack us in the face.

"I don't know," said Bree. "I don't think it would affect my life that much. Unless, God forbid, she took an interest in me." She pretended to shudder, and I couldn't help laughing—the first time in days.

"Oi, Morgan," said a voice, and a chill hit me that had nothing to do with the weather. Killian, my half brother, was sitting on a stone bench at the edge of the school property.

Our eyes met, and he grinned at me, his attractive, somewhat feral grin. "You rang? It was you, right?"

Bree glanced at me, and I realized she didn't know I had called Killian here. I had told her about my experiences in New York: that Ciaran was my father, Killian my half brother, and why that meant I had to break up with Hunter. Bree had been incredibly supportive over the last few days, but I knew Killian's presence must have been a shock to her. Hell, it was a shock to me. Somehow I'd thought I would have more time to prepare. With him here, the wheels had to be set in motion, and I felt afraid.

I drew in a deep breath. "Hey, Killian," I said. "I was hoping to talk to you again."

"At your disposal." He spread his arms wide. His English accent was adorable. I hadn't seen him since I'd learned we were half siblings, and now I stared at him, trying to see some resemblance.

"Killian!" called Raven.

I groaned inwardly as she hurried over to us. In New York she had flirted with Killian hard and heavy and in front of Sky, who had not been amused. Somehow I hadn't factored Raven into the scheme of things when I had agreed to be part of Eoife's plan.

"Hey, baby!" she said enthusiastically, leaning down to kiss him on both cheeks. Killian looked happy to see another of his many admirers, and he pulled her down to sit next to him.

"I was nearby, thought I'd drop in," said Killian, giving me a glance. He knew that I was a blood witch and that the others weren't, and he seemed to be gauging what to say. Amusement lit his eyes.

"I'm so glad you did," purred Raven. "I thought we'd never see you again."

"Yet here I am," he said magnanimously. He smiled at her, and though I felt exasperated—*Go away, Raven*—I also couldn't help being amused, even a little proud. Killian was definitely fun to be around—but even more, I felt a sort of kinship to him. I understood his humor, and his party-guy act didn't bother me like it did so many of the others. Maybe that's what blood ties really felt like.

"And here *you* are," he said to Bree, checking her out in a way that was so outrageous, it was funny. She gave him a skeptical smile, then turned away.

"I'm starving," she said, turning her gaze to me. "Want to go get something to eat?"

I bit my lip. Now that Killian was here, it was time to bond with him—time to gain his trust, ask about Ciaran, and hopefully get Ciaran out here. "Um, actually . . . Killian and I need to catch up."

Bree looked surprised. "Oh." She glanced over at Killian, who seemed absorbed with Raven, and then whispered to me, "Is everything okay?"

"Yes," I said. "I'm sorry, Bree. I just need some time to talk to Killian."

Bree nodded slowly. "You'll be all right alone with him?" she whispered.

I nodded quickly and circled my thumb and forefinger in the "okay" sign.

Bree nodded again, but her eyes still shone with concern. "All right," she said, loud enough for Killian and Raven to hear. "Well, I'm going to head home. See you guys."

"Oh, yes, you certainly will." Killian turned and grinned

suggestively, and Bree smiled in a sort of confused way as she headed off.

"Well, I'm up for anything, as always," Killian said, standing up and turning to me so that Raven's leg was pushed to the side. "Though I should mention that I'm rather famished myself."

"I know a diner we could go to."

"Perfect!" Killian flashed his trademark grin and turned to Raven. "How about you, love? Care to join us?"

"I can't," Raven said, frowning. "Mom's suing Dad again and I have to meet with the lawyers." She rolled her eyes. "They are such losers."

"Oh, too bad," I said, relieved, as Killian and I headed for Das Boot. I wasn't sure if she meant the lawyers or her parents—probably both—and I didn't care. Killian waved behind him as we walked off.

"Cool car," he said as he climbed in, putting his arm across the back of the bench seat. "I love huge American cars. Gas-guzzlers." He smiled. "What year?"

"Nineteen seventy-one," I said, pulling out into the street and heading toward the highway. Despite having called him, I was still rattled by Killian's presence, and the weight of my mission pressed in on my chest, making me feel like I had drunk a couple of double espressos. "Listen, Killian," I added quickly, "do you know who I am?" Might as well plunge right in.

"Sure. The witch from New York. With the friends, at the club." He slouched comfortably against the seat, unconcerned that he was in a car with a virtual stranger going to a place he didn't know, in a town he had just shown up in. He seemed like a leaf, a colorful autumn leaf, tossed about by the wind and content to go where it took him.

I took a deep breath. "Ciaran MacEwan is your father."

He straightened a tiny bit, and I felt tension entering his body. He took a longer look at me, and I felt him cast his senses toward me, trying to figure out if I was friend or foe. I blocked his scan easily, not letting him in, and saw him straighten more.

"Yeah," he answered warily. "You knew that. So?"

My throat constricted as I turned onto the access road to Highway 9. Somehow I just couldn't get the words out, and suddenly the diner was there in front of us. I pulled in and parked, and we didn't speak again until we had ordered.

The waitress brought our drinks. We sat across from each other in the back booth of the fifties-retro diner. Killian took the paper off his straw, stuck it in his chocolate milk shake, and sipped—all without taking his eyes off me. I watched him, unable to decide what my next move should be.

"So, what do you want with Ciaran? Is your seeker boyfriend looking for him?" Killian finally said lightly, but his face didn't match his voice.

I fought to hide my surprise at his question. "The Seeker is not my boyfriend," I said, looking him in the eye. "I found out Ciaran MacEwan is my father, too."

Killian sat back as if he'd been slapped. His eyes open wide, he scanned me again, looking at my hair, my eyes, my face.

"I realized it in New York," I explained awkwardly. "I didn't know until then. But—Ciaran and my mother had an affair, and my mother had me." And they were mùirn beatha dàns, soul mates, and then Ciaran killed her. And a short while ago he tried to kill me. I wondered if Killian had any idea what had happened to me in New York. I figured the odds were against it—he had told me that he and Ciaran weren't all that close.

Appearing out of nowhere, the waitress clanked our plates onto the table in front of us. Killian and I both jumped. After she left, he continued to look at me, stroking his chin.

"What was her name?" he asked finally. "Your mother."

"Maeve Riordan, of Belwicket."

I might as well have said Joan of Arc or Queen Elizabeth. He stared at me as if I'd suddenly grown two heads.

"I know that name," he said faintly. Then, seeming to come back to himself, he shook his head and looked down at his hamburger. "American hamburgers." He sighed happily. "I'm so sick of mad cow disease." He picked it up with both hands and took a big bite, closing his eyes in pleasure.

Now what? How did I get from here to having him tell me everything about Ciaran and getting Ciaran to come to Widow's Vale? Somehow I had to find a way. Every day, every hour counted. At this very minute Alyce was at Practical Magick, feeling a heavy mantle of doom lowering over her head.

"How did you find out about Ciaran?" Killian asked after a minute, taking another bite. Apparently discovering he had a half sister hadn't dulled his appetite.

"I've read Maeve's Book of Shadows," I said. "She talks about Ciaran in it. Then in New York, I sort of—got in trouble. Ciaran helped me get out of it. And we figured out how we knew each other . . . that he was my father. I—I have his eyes."

"Yes, you do," Killian said, studying my face.

"Anyway," I went on. "He helped me, and he's my biological father. I didn't get a chance to really talk to him in New York or even thank him." I shrugged and glanced up to find Killian looking at me intently, and I felt a surprising strength coming from him.

"But you weren't raised by Maeve," Killian said quietly. "You couldn't have been. How did you come to be here, in Widow's Vale?"

"Maeve put me up for adoption," I explained. "My family, the Rowlandses, adopted me. They're the only parents I've ever known. I have a sister, but not a blood sister, of course. I mean, when I realized who Ciaran was and that you were his son, I realized that I had an actual half brother . . . by blood." Mary K., please forgive me.

Killian blinked, as if this notion were just occurring to him. He focused on his food, working his way through his burger and shake with steady intent.

As the minutes went by, I felt more and more anxious. What if Killian hated me, the flesh-and-blood evidence of his father betraying his mother? At last he looked up, his plate completely clean. He smiled.

"Well! A little sister," he said cheerfully. "Brilliant. I always hated being the baby." He stood and leaned across the table to kiss me on the cheek. "Welcome to the family." He made a rueful face. "Such as it is. Now. What do they have for pudding here?"

I watched as Killian devoured a slab of chocolate silk pie, and the new silence felt awkward. I studied Killian, trying to think, trying to prod my addled brain into motion. I needed information from him. That was why he was here. I needed to know everything he could tell me.

"Was Ciaran a . . . good father?" I asked.

"Not particularly," Killian said, sitting sideways on his bench and putting his feet up. "He wasn't around a lot, you know. He and Mum hate each other. He used to come around a couple of times a year, and he would test us kids and find us all wanting and blame my mother, and she'd cry, and then he'd take off."

"That isn't how I pictured it at all," I said. "I thought, he's your real father. He would teach you. He would show you magick. I thought you were so lucky to have him around."

"Nope." Killian seemed unconcerned, but I could tell it was a facade. "What about you? How's your dad?"

"Great," I said. "He's really brilliant—does all sorts of research and design and experiments. But then he'll leave his glasses in the fridge, and forget to put gas in his car, so it runs out, and you'll ask him to get something and find him an hour later, reading in his office."

Killian laughed. "But he's nice?"

"Really nice. He loves me a lot."

"There you go, then." Killian rubbed his hands together and looked up, as if to say, Shall we go?

"It must be difficult for you," I said quickly, trying to keep this conversation going. "I mean . . . I hope you're not upset with me. For bringing you here. For springing all this stuff on you so quickly."

Killian looked surprised for a moment, and then he seemed to regard me differently. He gave a rueful smile. "Well, love, it's not as though my family life has been *The Cosby Show*. Finding out that I have a little sister . . ." He seemed to take me in, and at that moment I felt a sense of connection to him, like this wasn't just an awkward conversation between strangers. I sensed in him that—kinship, I guess—that sprang from this less-than-ideal connection by blood. ". . . well, there are worse ways to spend a Monday afternoon."

I smiled in response, and immediately started to feel guilty about using Killian to get through to Ciaran. It saddened me to think that he was a real person, my real half brother, with feelings, and I was really only getting to know him as part of a spy maneuver. The fate of Starlocket was a pretty good motivation, but I was beginning to feel that I liked Killian and that I might enjoy getting to know him even if Ciaran weren't involved.

"So do you and Ciaran ever . . . see each other?"

Killian made a face as though he tasted something sour and took a last sip of chocolate shake. "No." He shifted, and I realized all at once that he was incredibly uncomfortable with this conversation and wanted to flee. "I'm beat, sis," he said as I kicked myself mentally for not changing the subject earlier. "It was lovely speaking with you. I'll see you around."

"But—" I watched helplessly as Killian left some money on the table and walked briskly out the door. "Killian! Wait!" I threw some money down on top of Killian's, grabbed my stuff, and ran out the door behind him. How would he get home? We were too far from anything to walk. Widow's Vale wasn't exactly a place where you could just hail a taxi.

But I didn't see Killian in the parking lot, and a quick scan of the highway found no pedestrians, no cars headed in either direction. In fact, I realized, I hadn't heard a car go by in the last five minutes or so. I looked back at the parking lot, moving closer to study the woods on the perimeter of the lot. There were no footprints anywhere; the ground looked untouched by human feet. Frustrated, I leaned against Das Boot and took a last look around. Where had he *gone?* Had he actually used magick just to get away from me?

Finally, after a few more minutes trying to make sense of

it, I climbed into Das Boot, checking my watch. Five o'clock. Barely twenty-four hours after accepting Eoife's mission, and I was already feeling pretty certain that I had just ruined the council's plan.

Eoife was staying at Hunter and Sky's, and Hunter answered the phone when I called. The sound of his voice made my heart flutter inside my chest, but I ruthlessly pushed down the pain. "Hunter? I need to talk to Eoife."

"What's wrong?" Hunter's voice was warm with concern. Oh, Goddess, I thought, I can't talk to you about how I've already ruined everything.

"Um—Killian's here. But he kind of . . . got away."

"Got *away*?" Some of the warmth leached out of his voice, and I sucked in my breath to prepare for his disappointment.

"Well—"

"Listen, Eoife just walked in." Hunter cut me off. "I'll put her on."

Before I could react, Hunter was gone from the line and I heard Eoife's voice. "Morgan? Is there a problem?"

"Well," I began, "Killian came, and we were talking, but he took off before I could talk to him about calling Ciaran. And then he sort of . . . disappeared, and now I don't know where he is or when I'll see him again."

"Morgan, calm down. It's not a disaster." Eoife's sensible voice, if not exactly warm, still calmed my nerves a bit. "Listen, I was just heading out to attend a Starlocket circle. Would you like to meet me there?"

Starlocket? Oh, no. How could I face Alyce and all of the innocent members of Starlocket when I might have just thrown away their one chance for survival?

"I don't know, Eoife. I mean . . . maybe this mission isn't for me. Maybe you should find someone who's better equipped—"

"Morgan," Eoife interrupted me, "I think you're overreacting. Come with me to the circle—it will calm you down. And we can talk a bit about how to approach Killian from now on."

I sighed. It *would* calm me to attend a circle, especially since I'd skipped Kithic's this week. And Alyce was always a warm and comforting presence—I could only hope that no harm would come to her anytime soon. "All right," I said finally. "Where is it?"

Starlocket was meeting at a cozy, cedar-shingled house on the outskirts of town. When I rang the doorbell, the door was answered by a tall, formidable woman who looked to be in her late thirties. She had long, dark brown hair that reached all the way down to her butt, and she wore a brilliant robe of purple silk. "Hello," she greeted me.

"Hi," I said. "I'm Morgan Rowlands. I'm a friend of Alyce and Eoife's."

"It's nice to meet you, Morgan." The woman regarded me calmly. "Welcome to my home. I'm Suzanna Mearis." Suzanna stepped back from the doorway and gestured into a small living room. "The circle will be held in here. Eoife hasn't arrived yet."

I thanked Suzanna and headed past her into the warm, golden-hued room. Nature-themed oil paintings adorned the walls in shades of green, gold, orange, and red. A rust-colored velvet couch sat before a brick fireplace, and candles burned on every available surface. Several members of the coven were sitting on the couch, chatting, and I noticed Alyce standing by a window, looking out into the night. I walked over to her. "Alyce?" I said softly. She turned and hugged me tightly without a word.

"Morgan," she whispered finally. "I'm so happy you've come."

"It's good to be here." Seeing Alyce made me realize how much I'd missed my friend and confidante, and I had to fight back tears.

Alyce's eyes met mine, and I could see her concern shining there. Her voice dropped. "I know that you had a difficult time in New York."

A difficult time, I thought. Difficult was right. One blessing of this new assignment was that it kept my mind off just how much my life had changed in the last week. I nodded, not feeling up to talking about it just now, even to Alyce.

"Morgan?" I felt a hand on my shoulder and turned to find Eoife in a green linen robe. "We should talk."

I nodded and followed Eoife to a private corner of the room, after saying good-bye to Alyce, and promising we'd get together as soon as possible.

"Listen," Eoife began, "Killian isn't going to open up to you right away. What we've asked you to do is get close to him, and that's going to take more than just one meeting. Given what we know about Killian's upbringing, I can imagine that he doesn't trust people too easily. If you were able to make contact and tell him who you are, you should consider this first meeting successful."

She had a point, I realized, but I hadn't counted on my half brother disappearing into the blue. "But how can I be sure there'll be a next meeting?" I asked. "I have no idea where Killian went or how he got there. And he's not answering my witch messages."

Eoife put her hand on my shoulder. "Morgan, remember: Killian is your half brother. He may not want to share everything with you right away, but we believe that he will feel a connection to you and that he will want to meet with you again. You just have to give him time."

I sighed. I didn't have time. Starlocket didn't have time. "What if I scried for him?" I asked hopefully. "I've always had good luck scrying with fire. I could find out where Ciaran is, what he's up to—"

"Absolutely not," Eoife said instantly. "What's most important right now is to keep Ciaran and Killian's trust. You don't want to scare them off with a lot of questions at once or by letting them know that you're watching them. Once Killian gets to know you, the subject of Ciaran will inevitably come up. But for now, as hard as it is, you just have to be patient."

I nodded reluctantly. "I understand," I said quietly. "I'm just . . . scared." I looked over to where the coven was gathering. I couldn't bear knowing that I'd failed to save them.

"Being afraid is natural, Morgan." Eoife followed my gaze to the coven members. "But you mustn't allow that fear to drive Killian away."

An hour later I no longer felt afraid. Joined with Eoife and the members of Starlocket, I swirled ecstatically in our circle, feeling my magick course through me in a way that made me feel powerful, unstoppable. The fire in the fireplace glowed orange and blue, and I was a part of that fire: fire was my partner, and together we were capable of anything. I would see Killian again, I felt sure. The power in me could not be contained. I would help Starlocket any way I could.

Then, suddenly, everything changed. There were other

voices in the room, voices that didn't belong to any of the members of Starlocket. They were lower, harsher, inhuman. Slowly they began to get louder, until they were almost shouting. They were chanting words I didn't recognize, but the mere sound of them made my skin crawl. The voices built to a crescendo, and suddenly the fire sputtered and was gone. The circle stopped moving. Through my haze of magick I saw somebody falling to the floor. A sudden shock of fear ran through me, like ice water pumping through my heart.

I dropped to my knees and closed my eyes, and I could feel the magick running out of my body. I remembered the first few times I felt my magick, before I understood what it was. The feeling was overwhelming, and sometimes the power of it made me sick. I wondered if somehow I had lost control again. Slowly, painfully, I opened my eyes.

Before me on the floor lay Suzanna Mearis. Alyce was bent over her.

"Someone help me carry her to her room," Alyce commanded. Her face was drawn. Suddenly she looked haggard.

I felt a welling of fear. "What happened?" I asked. "What's wrong with her?"

Eoife was the one who answered me. "A taibhs came," she said in a hushed voice. "More than one, I'd say. Dark spirits. They broke through all our protections and attacked the circle. Suzanna took the brunt of the attack. We were able to banish them, but . . ."

"Is she okay?" I asked in a near whisper. "Will she be okay?"

Eoife's face was somber. "I hope so, Morgan. But I just don't know."

6.
Forbidden Magick

There is a villager here named Nuala. Without the abbot's permission I asked to meet with her, as she was one of the few Wodebaynes who would meet my eyes.

I asked her frankly what deviltry was at work here. She said no deviltry at all since there was no devil. I cried out that that was heresy and that if she had no fear of the eternal fires of hell, how could she hope to join our Lord in heaven? Brother Colin, she laughed and said there was no heaven, either. As I gaped in horror, she leaned close so I could smell heather and smoke in her hair. She said, "I'll fill your cow's udder if you kiss me."

I turned and ran. Surely, Brother Colin, this Nuala Riordan is the devil's own agent.

—Brother Sinestus Tor, to Colin, May 1768

By the time I left Suzanna Mearis's house that night, she was still unconscious, and Alyce had finally made the decision to call an ambulance. Whatever had happened to Suzanna, she wasn't waking up. We could only pray that the doctors at the local hospital might be able to offer some help.

I spent the rest of the night wide awake in my bed, terrified by every little sound I heard. Tuesday was another meaningless day: moving through classes, lunch, classes, without any of it registering. It was endless and foggy, clouded by my worries for Suzanna and the possibility of more dark presences to come, not to mention my misery over Hunter and the deep dread I had of failing Starlocket. Eleven days, I kept thinking miserably. I had eleven days before all of Starlocket was hit by something even stronger than what had happened to Suzanna.

When the final bell rang, I shuffled out with the other students, lost in thought.

"Hey, sis." My head snapped up at the voice.

"Killian!" I couldn't believe he had come back after yesterday. As I walked toward the stone bench, I felt a renewed sense of purpose: today I would get useful information out of him. Yes, I liked him. But I had to save Starlocket. And my time was running out.

An hour later I was sitting at a huge table in a local chain restaurant, feeling more relaxed than I had in days. We were a huge party, with emphasis on the word *party.* While I had been talking to Killian at school, he had managed to charm all the other Widow's Vale High members of Kithic, including Alisa Soto, who had never joined us on the basement steps before. Now we were sitting at four tables pushed together, eating potato skins, fried mozzarella sticks, popcorn shrimp—every kind of appetizer on the menu.

Killian was the center of attention—right now he was in the middle of a story about magick gone wrong—"Oh,

Goddess, and there I was in that field, with a flipping angry bull, and me in my robe and nothing else. . . ."

Bree was laughing, leaning against Robbie. She hadn't been impressed with Killian in New York, but she seemed to have accepted him now that she knew he was my half brother. Anyway, I was glad that Bree hadn't been attracted to Killian. In the past, she had always gone after whoever she wanted and had always gotten them—except Cal. But she was definitely not flirting with Killian, and she had deliberately sat next to Robbie at the table. True, Robbie was better looking than Killian. But then, Robbie was better looking than most guys.

Raven was another matter. If Sky could see her with Killian's hands all over her, well, it could get pretty ugly. With any luck, Sky wouldn't find out.

"Pass the salt, please," Matt said. He had been smiling and chuckling tonight for the first time in months.

"Cheers," Killian said, and looked at the saltshaker. It began to slide quickly down the tables, hopping over the cracks between them, and stopped in front of Matt. After a moment of surprise I gave in to the fun and giggled at this casual show of magick. Everyone else laughed and seemed to admire Killian's power, and he basked in the attention like a sunflower.

"Too much," Jenna laughed, her face flushed and pretty. Matt's dark eyes met hers, and she looked away.

"What do you think, sis?" Killian asked me. "Do *you* think it's too much?" His smile was wide, his face open, but I sensed a challenge there. Was this a test?

I shook my head. "No. But *this* might be too much." Remembering what I had done on Saturday, I concentrated on the saltshaker. Light as air, I thought, and then the shaker rose slowly off the table. Everyone went quiet in surprise. Quickly I lowered the shaker, feeling my face color with self-consciousness. Everyone was staring at me, and I felt Alisa's huge dark eyes on me, as if she was afraid. I shouldn't have done that, I realized. It was too much, especially for a public place. Why did I feel like I had to impress Killian?

"I didn't know you were initiated," Killian said.

"I'm not. I just—" I shrugged.

Robbie was looking at me. I couldn't meet his gaze, I knew what I'd see there: the lack of trust I'd seen in his eyes in New York.

Bree was staring at me, too. "You *move* things?" she demanded. "You *levitate* things?"

"Uh, just recently," I said, feeling guilty. Hunter would so kill me if he had seen that. Speaking of Hunter, I realized that I should probably tell him where I was. After what had happened last night, the seriousness of our situation seemed much more real.

"Why did you call Morgan sis?" Matt asked. My stomach fell. I didn't know if I was ready to deal with Kithic knowing that we were half siblings.

Killian grinned broadly and stretched his arm across the back of my chair. "Oh, you know—Morgan and I, we're kindred spirits."

Startled, I caught Killian's eye, and he winked.

"You and *Morgan?*" Robbie looked at me questioningly, and when I shrugged, he gave me one of his skeptical half smiles. "Whatever you say. . . ."

"Can I borrow your phone? I was supposed to call Eileen," I asked Bree. She took out her tiny red cell phone and handed it to me. I got up and moved ten feet away.

I punched in Hunter's phone number from memory. Crap! His phone was busy. Get call waiting, I thought. I'd have to try him again later.

"Hey, I know what," Killian was saying as I returned to the table. "I found a pub over in Nortonville. What say we adjourn there?" Nortonville was a slightly bigger town about twenty minutes away.

"Ooh, yeah," said Raven at once.

"I'm up for it," Bree said, glancing at her watch. It wasn't eight yet. She looked at Robbie, and he nodded at her.

In the end everyone but Alisa, who asked to be dropped off at home, claiming that she needed to cram for a geometry test, piled into three cars and drove over to Nortonville. I was in front, with Matt's white pickup and Breezy, Bree's BMW, behind me. Jenna, Ethan, and Sharon were laughing in the backseat of my car. Next to me, Killian was humming cheerfully and keeping time by hitting his knee with his palm.

My brain was already in the pub, trying to plan a way to get closer to Killian. If Killian started drinking, maybe he would let something slip. Maybe then it would be easier to talk to him about Ciaran, ask him to get Ciaran to come to Widow's Vale. Tonight was the night to get him to open up. Eoife had made sense last night, but right now Suzanna Mearis lay in a coma. Every time I thought of Imbolc and the remaining members that could be hurt before then, I felt sick. Time was all too short.

"Turn down this road," Killian directed.

"Oh, this is old Highway 60," I realized. "We're not quite in Nortonville. We come down this road to get to the mall."

Killian shrugged. "Up there." He pointed. "There it is."

When Killian had said "pub," I had pictured a publike restaurant, maybe with an Olde English theme. But this was an actual bar. It was called the Twilite, and it looked like a converted Dairy Queen with its windows painted over and red lightbulbs blinking out front.

The three cars parked, and we gathered in the cold night air.

"So, Killian," said Jenna. "How do we plan to get in? We're all underage."

"Not a problem," Killian said lightly. "Leave it to me."

From the corner of my eye, I saw Sharon and Ethan having a whispered conference. In the end Sharon sighed, and they joined us by the bar's door. It was a Tuesday, so there were only a few other cars in the lot. The battered pink door opened, and a big guy leaned out to look at us.

"Yeah?"

Here's where we get bounced, I thought, but Killian looked at the guy and said quietly, "There are nine of us."

The man frowned and glanced at us. Killian waited patiently, and when the bouncer looked back at Killian, he seemed confused for a moment. "Right, nine," he said finally, as if from a distance.

Killian smiled broadly, clapped the bouncer on the back, and strode into the bar. The rest of us followed him like baby ducks. Inside it was dark and smelled like spilled beer and sawdust and fried food. With my magesight I could see clearly at once, but Bree and Robbie hesitated next to me. I touched Bree's arm lightly, and she followed me deeper into the Twilite.

"And another Jell-O shot for me and my friend!" Killian called loudly.

The waitress smiled and nodded and headed to the bar. It was ten-thirty, and the Twilite had picked up a lot.

"This place isn't so bad," Bree said loudly into my ear. Music was streaming from the old-fashioned jukebox that Killian kept feeding with quarters. By now we were all used to the noise and the dim light and the flickering of a TV that was mounted high in one corner. There were two pool tables in an alcove in back, and a group of townies was playing and getting progressively louder.

I nodded in agreement. "It looks like a dive from outside." This felt similar to being with Killian in that club in New York, except this place was smaller, much less cool, and much less crowded. And of course, this place wasn't packed with blood witches. And Hunter and I were no longer together. . . . Oh, Goddess, don't go down that road, I told myself. Still, the festive air that surrounded my half brother had caught up to us in the Twilite, and once again we were all laughing until our faces hurt, even me. The fact that most of us were drinking, underage or not, wasn't hurting.

"Hey, are you all right?" Bree spoke into my ear again, struggling to be heard over the music but still be quiet enough so the whole pub wouldn't hear. "I know it must be hard for you, being out but not having Hunter anymore."

I nodded. I was grateful for Bree's concern, but this didn't seem like the time or place to talk about it. "It's hard," I agreed. "Thanks for asking. I'm okay, though."

"If you ever need to talk . . ." Robbie came up behind Bree and kissed her cheek. She giggled, and suddenly I felt very single. Bree gave me one last concerned look, and I smiled to show her I was okay.

"Sip?" Bree asked Robbie, holding out her screwdriver.

He shook his head, half smiling. "No—some of us have to be able to drive." Bree was being extremely friendly to him, pressing close and talking in his ear. I looked around the table, feeling like everyone here was my good friend, that we could all trust each other and that we could celebrate Wicca together. Not having Hunter with me, being a single girl among all the couples—I missed what I'd had with Hunter more than I could say. But still, having a group of friends I loved helped ease the pain inside me, just a little.

Jenna, on her third beer, giggled and leaned against Sharon, who wasn't drinking at all. She looked like she wasn't having as good a time as the rest of us. Ethan wasn't drinking, either, but he'd been getting twitchier and twitchier, and I wondered if they'd had a fight. To keep everyone else company, I had ordered a whiskey sour, which was what my mom usually drank. It hadn't been too bad, and I had ordered another. Killian and Raven had downed so many Jell-O shots that I had lost count. Now seemed a good time to talk to him. Smiling at him, I edged closer.

"Killian, I wanted to ask you—" I began.

"I love this song!" Killian shouted as the jukebox started another number. "Come on!" Clambering out of our booth, he grabbed Bree's hand, who grabbed Robbie's hand, who grabbed my hand, and then we were all dancing together on the tiny dance floor with sawdust slipping under our feet. And my opportunity was lost.

I've never been a big partyer, and I hate dancing in public. The thing about whiskey sours, though, is they make you mind that kind of stuff less. Back at the table, Sharon and Ethan were actually bickering. When Ethan grabbed a beer off the waitress's tray, Sharon's face set like cement, and she grabbed her purse. I saw her ask Matt to take her home, and he agreed, shooting Ethan a glance.

"Do you want me to come with you?" Jenna said, and though I couldn't hear the words physically, I heard them in my mind. Sharon shrugged, looking upset, and Jenna got her coat and followed Sharon and Matt. Ethan was sucking down his beer, watching Sharon angrily, but he didn't stop her from leaving. In moments he had finished the first beer and started on another.

"What was that about?" I asked Robbie. He and I had edged away from the crowd and were now leaning against a back wall that felt sticky. I felt hot and out of breath, and a third whiskey sour felt fabulous going down my throat.

"Ethan had stopped drinking," Robbie told me, not looking happy. "I don't think it was a great idea for him to come here."

"Oh, crap," I said, my head feeling light.

Robbie shrugged. At the table, Ethan's second beer was empty. He signaled for another, but the waitress tapped her watch.

"Good," I said, setting my empty glass on top of the jukebox. "It's closing time. They'll cut him off, and we can go home." I staggered a bit when I pushed myself off the wall, and that seemed amusing. It took forever for us to get our coats and scarves and hats and gloves and pay our check, which was a truly stunning amount. Bree put it on her credit card, and we all promised to pay her back.

The shock of the night air took my breath away. "Oh, it's beautiful out," I said, gesturing to the wide expanse of sky.

The night seemed darker than usual, the stars brighter. But looking up made me lose my balance, and I would have fallen over if I hadn't crashed into Killian.

Laughing, he held me up until I was steady, and I blinked at him as the realization slowly came to me: I was wasted.

Robbie was loading Bree and Ethan into Breezy, and they were both feeling no pain. Raven was plastering herself to Killian, kissing him good-bye, and he wasn't resisting.

"Take me home," she said softly, holding his face between her hands. I rolled my eyes and started pawing through my fanny pack for my keys. Do not go home with her, I thought. Sky will kill you. And I need to talk to you alone. With a sudden pang, I wished Hunter were here. He would know what to do. He would help me. I would feel so much better.

"Raven, come on with us," Robbie said. My hero. "You live close to Ethan, and I can drop you off. Morgan takes another exit."

"I want to go home with you," Raven told Killian. She pressed her hips against him and smiled. "And you want me to."

He laughed and disengaged himself easily. "Not tonight, Raven. I'll take a rain check."

For a moment Raven couldn't decide whether to be angry or to pout, but in the end she was too drunk for either and fell backward into the backseat of Bree's car. Robbie sighed and slammed the door shut. Bree's fine dark hair was pressed against her window, and I saw her eyes were closed. With a wave good-bye, Robbie started Breezy and drove off.

"Fun people, your friends," said Killian. His words came out with puffs of condensation.

I looked at him for a moment until I understood the actual words. "Uh-huh," I said stupidly.

Killian grinned with delight and brushed my damp hair off my neck. "Little sister, are you tipsy?"

"I'm a mess," I said, feeling like my tongue needed to lie down and rest. Then two more synapses fired. "Oh, crap!" I said. "We're both drunk. Who's going to drive? We'll have to call a taxi."

"Oh, love, you're so concerned with what's right and wrong," Killian said soothingly. "It'll be fine. You know these roads. This car's a tank. No worries."

I was so drunk that I almost believed him. Then I shook my head, which felt loose and floppy. "No. We can't drive drunk," I slurred. "That—*that* would be bad."

His dark eyes glittered in the night.

I'm related to him, I thought in a daze. We share the same blood. I have a brother.

Slowly Killian reached out again and spread his hand on the side of my head, pushing his fingers beneath my hair. Smiling down at me, he whispered some words in Gaelic that I didn't know but somehow understood the meaning of. I started to feel strange and closed my eyes. When he quit speaking, I waited till he had moved his hand, then opened my eyes. I felt stone-cold sober.

I looked around. I felt completely normal. I could walk, talk, and think. Killian saw the comprehension on my face and laughed again, his white teeth gleaming against his lips.

"Okay, I can drive," I said.

We got into Das Boot, my brain clicking away efficiently. I was sober; Killian was plastered. And I was going to find out where he was staying. There were possibilities here. I might get some information from him after all.

I drove slowly back down old Highway 60. Killian was leaning against his door, his head against the window. Eyes closed, he was singing under his breath.

"How did you get home last night?" I asked. "I ran after you to offer you a ride home, but you were already gone. How'd you do it?"

Killian was looking out the window, not at me, but I could still sense his mischievous smile. "Oh, didn't you see, love?" he asked. "I had my portable broomstick in my pocket."

All right, I thought. I took that as something that I shouldn't press further. Let's try a new tactic.

"Where am I taking you now? Where are you staying?"

"Oh, ah . . ." Killian peered out the window, as if trying to figure it out himself. "I don't really know the names of the roads here. I'll just have to tell you where to turn. You stay on this road for a while."

Okay. "You and Ciaran don't seem that much alike," I said, keeping my eyes on the road.

He blinked sleepily, giving me a sweet smile. I could see how he would be popular anywhere he went. He was fun, undemanding, flexible, and not at all mean-spirited.

"No," he agreed. "We're not."

"Is that because he just wasn't around that much when you were little?"

Killian thought. "Maybe. Partly. But it's the whole nature-and-nurture thing. Even if he'd been around all the time, signing my school mark report, I'd probably still be pretty different from him."

"Why?" Note to self: Do not become a lawyer. Your interrogation skills suck.

He shrugged. "Don't know." He sat up in his seat. "Take a left here."

So he wasn't Mr. Introspection. Okay. New tactic. "What are your brother and sister like?"

"They're different from him, too. I don't know." Killian looked out the window into the dark woods on his side of the car. There was no moon tonight; the sky was laden with heavy clouds that seemed almost to touch the treetops. "It's just—Da is very ambitious, you know? He married Mum so he could lead her mother's coven. He just wants power, no matter what. It's more important than family or . . ." His voice trailed off, and I wondered if he thought he'd said too much. He still seemed very drunk—his words were thick and seemed to take a lot of thought.

"Is your mom like that, too?"

Killian gave a short bark of a laugh. "Goddess, no. Which is why Da inherited her coven, not her. She should be really strong, it's in her blood, but she just pisses it all away, you know? Ma's a housewife, a princess, really. Always complaining about her lot in life. I think she loved Da, but he loved her inheritance. Plus she was pregnant with my older brother when they got married."

This picture of Ciaran's life seemed so different than what I'd imagined, reading the romantic, agonized entries in Maeve's BOS.

"Anyway—if he loved your ma, then maybe that explains why he couldn't stand any of us." There was a bewildered hurt in his voice that I didn't think would have been there without all the Jell-O shots.

"I'm sorry, Killian," I said, and meant it. In his own way, he was another of Ciaran's victims. Did everyone Ciaran touched pay a price for it? Did I have the same effect?

"Yeah, well." Killian gave a smile. "I don't lose sleep over it. But I don't want you to think you're inheriting Mr. and Mrs. Lovely. Our family's kind of different." He gave what seemed like a bitter chuckle and leaned his head against the window again.

"But they're still your family," I said. "They're yours. They belong to you and you to them. That's something." I wasn't aware of the tense catch in my throat until the final word and didn't turn around when I felt my half brother's eyes on me.

"Stop here a minute," he said.

"Here?" I looked out at the deserted road. We were in the middle of the woods; I couldn't see any houses anywhere. Why did he want me to stop?

"Right here." I stopped the car, and Killian leaned over and kissed me on the cheek. It was very gentle and grape flavored. "Now you belong to us, too, little sister."

To avoid bursting into unexpected tears, I opened my door and got out, standing next to Das Boot in the dark night. Killian got out also, clumsily hanging on to the car door to avoid falling down. He started laughing at himself, and I smiled.

"Look, sis," he said, gesturing at the sky. He looked at me with mischief glittering in his eyes. "Repeat after me: grenlach altair dan, buren nitha sentac." Watching his face, I repeated the words, imitating his pronunciation as best I could. They sounded much better with his accent, but when he went on, I followed, feeling the thin coil of magick awakening within me. What were we doing?

He was watching the sky, and I was, too, not knowing what to look for. Then Killian waved his right hand in a smooth, sweeping gesture, oddly graceful, and I saw the heavy clouds overhead parting reluctantly to reveal the clear, star-speckled sky behind them. My mouth went slack as I realized what he had done.

"Now you." He tapped my hand, and disbelieving, I moved it in a gentle circle before me. The clouds above moved at my command, and with a broader movement I pushed the huge billows aside. All was clear above us. Weather magick was forbidden; it was considered an assault on nature and could have far-reaching, devastating effects. So I had just worked forbidden magick. And I had loved it.

My heart was pounding with excitement, and I looked at Killian, my eyes wide and shining. He laughed at my expression.

"Don't say I never gave you anything," he said. "I gave you the stars. Good night, little sister."

He started to walk away, weaving slightly down the dark road.

"Good night? Where are you going?" I yelled. "This is the middle of nowhere!"

He turned and gave me a mock-severe look. "Everyplace is somewhere. I want to walk from here." He turned and began to walk away again.

"But—" I stared at him, feeling something close to panic. "Killian! Wait!"

He turned again from the woods and looked at me. I took a deep breath. "I want to see Ciaran again. Can you ask him to come here, to see me?" There. It was out. I had said it.

For a moment Killian was silent, then his faint laughter floated to me just as a glowing sliver of moon appeared in the clouds' clearing. "I'll think about it," he called back. Then he was gone, into the nothingness, and I was left alone in the cold, wondering whether I had actually succeeded in my mission—or whether Killian was just playing with me the same way he played with the clouds.

7. Witch Fire

Brother Thomas's wound continues to fester. He is near delirium, and I fear he will lose the leg. Brother Colin, I must set this letter aside; Father Benedict has motioned to me. I will finish later.

The Lord works in mysterious ways. Father Benedict came to me in all gravity and voiced his concern about Brother Thomas. He commanded me to go seek help from a village granny-wife. I asked if that was not like asking for help from the devil, to which he replied that God judges what is good or evil, not man.

In the village no granny-wife would see me, but Nuala Riordan came with me and is still with Brother Thomas. I tremble in fear for our very souls: she is chanting devil's words over him, fixing him foul teas, applying seaweed poultices to his wound. To my mind it would be better if he died rather than have the devil heal him.

—Brother Sinestus Tor, to Colin, June 1768

I pulled into our dark driveway and felt Das Boot's big engine stop with a tremble. What a night. It had been incredible. Now I had to go in and steel myself to call Eoife, to tell her I had asked Killian to call Ciaran.

I was almost to my front door, keys in hand, when suddenly every bit of alcohol I had drunk flooded back into my brain with a whoosh. I staggered on the walk, dumbfounded. Oh my God. Killian's spell had worn off—what if it had worn off while I was driving? Now I was completely polluted again.

Inside the house, I dumped my stuff on the floor and literally crawled upstairs to my room. How much had I drunk? More than I ever had in my life. My stomach felt iffy, and I began to regret downing those whiskey sours.

Ten minutes later I lay in my bed with the spins, wanting to cry. The room was rocking back and forth as if I were on a ship, my stomach felt extremely fragile, and I had to get up to go to school in about six hours.

A moment after that I realized that the dull, heavy pounding I felt in my head was really someone banging on my front door. Jesus, who could that be? I tried to focus my senses to cast them but couldn't concentrate. I was all over the place and starting to panic. Then I heard the front door open—had I locked it?—and footsteps thudding up the stairs.

"Morgan!" Hunter yelled, right before he opened the door to my room. I looked at him stupidly while he stormed over to loom above me in my bed. "Where the hell have you been? I sent you a witch message, I've been calling your house. Do you think this is a game? Do you think—"

"I tried to call you earlier!" I said, my voice sounding thick. "Your phone was busy!" Then, with a sickening rush, my stomach gave notice that it was about to rebel. I stared at Hunter in horror, then lunged toward the bathroom I shared with Mary K. I just barely made it to the toilet before everything I had eaten and drunk that evening came back up.

Throwing up is the most disgusting thing I can think of. I flushed the toilet after the first time, but then I vomited again and again, my stomach muscles heaving. I felt the little blood vessels around my eyes burst and wanted to cry but couldn't yet.

The only thing worse than barfing your guts up is doing it in front of someone you love desperately and are no longer with. I didn't hear him follow me, but my face crumpled with sobs when I felt Hunter's strong, gentle hands carefully lifting back my long hair. He twisted it away from my face while I was sick, and then when I sagged against the porcelain, he stepped away just long enough to wet a washcloth with cold water. He stroked it over my face as I sat mortified, humiliated tears filling my eyes.

"Oh, God," I muttered in misery.

"Can you stand up?" His anger had dissipated. I nodded, and Hunter helped me over to the sink, where I brushed my teeth three times, feeling shaky and hollow. He wet the washcloth again, gently pressing it against my face and the back of my neck under my hair. It felt incredible.

Feeling completely defeated and beyond any hope of redeeming myself, I shuffled back to my room and collapsed on my bed. That was when I realized I was wearing only the Wonder Woman undies Bree had given me months ago as a joke and my dad's threadbare MIT sweatshirt. Hunter was rooting through my dresser and finally found a long-sleeved rugby shirt that had seen too many washes. Businesslike, he came over, stripped off my sweatshirt, then popped the rugby shirt over my head, helping my arms find the sleeves.

Then he left my bedroom, and I slid sideways in my cool, comfortable bed, knowing my humiliation was now complete. Hunter and I had made out seriously before, and we'd put our hands under each other's shirts, but he'd never seen me practically naked until now. Now he had seen me in nothing but my Wonder Woman undies.

Hunter came back into my room, holding a cold can of ginger ale. He poured it into a glass and helped me sit up again so I could sip it. It was nirvana. "Thank you." My voice sounded harsh, scraped.

"So, you've been drinking a bit," he said unnecessarily, taking the glass from me and putting it on my bedside table.

I moaned pathetically, burying my face in my pillow. I still felt wretched but much, much better since my stomach had gotten rid of some of the poison in my system. The spins were gone, and the awful queasiness.

"Liquor dulls your senses," Hunter said mildly, stroking his hand down my hair, across my shoulder, down my side. I pulled the covers up past my waist. "It makes your magick go awry if you don't compensate for it. That's why most witches just have a little ceremonial wine, at most. . . ."

I started weeping, and he shut up. He didn't have to tell me this—I didn't want to drink again in my whole life. "I was with Killian tonight. He told me why Ciaran inherited his mother's coven and not her, but I didn't get anything else. But I did ask him to ask Ciaran to come here." Then I burst into tears, holding my pillow, feeling like I was releasing days' worth of tension, fear, and worry. Hunter sat close to me, his hand on my neck, smoothing my hair. He didn't say shhh or anything to make me stop crying but just waited while I got it out.

Finally I slowed down to shudders and hiccups. I gazed up at him through tear-blurred eyes, thinking how incredible he looked, how attractive and appealing and sexy and magickal, thinking about how wonderful and caring and thoughtful he had been tonight. My heart was breaking all over again. And here I was, having just been horribly sick in front of him, having him see me in my joke underwear and nothing else, and knowing that I looked like a total bowser when I cried. It was too much to bear, and I closed my eyes against the onslaught of emotional anguish that rushed over me.

"Tell me more about tonight, love," he said gently, leaning over me.

Slowly I reported everything that Killian and I had talked about. It seemed extremely thin. I was a failure. I talked about going to the bar tonight, and everyone drinking, and Ethan falling off the wagon. I confessed to Killian's working weather magick but not that I had done it also.

"Then right before he left me, I asked him to call Ciaran. He said he'd think about it."

"You did well," Hunter said. He looked at me and seemed about to say something but then decided against it. Instead he stroked my hair and down my back. I realized I was completely exhausted, hollowed out, wrung out, numb.

"Go to sleep," Hunter whispered.

"Mmm-hmm," I murmured, my eyes already closing.

"By the way," he said from the door, "nice knickers."

Then he was gone, and despite how horrible I felt at the

moment, I was smiling because I had seen his face, just for a little while.

The next afternoon Killian was waiting for me, the faithful spaniel, on his usual stone bench. It was odd—my heart was glad to see his smile. I was really beginning to like Killian. He was completely irresponsible and a bad influence, but nice. I immediately wanted to ask him about Ciaran—I was down to ten days now and Ciaran was nowhere in sight—but then I remembered Eoife's pep talk from the Starlocket circle. How pushy could I be without turning him off or making him suspicious? I decided to play it by ear.

He rubbed his hands together when he saw me walking toward him, Robbie and Bree in back of me. "What's up for tonight?"

"Anything that doesn't involve alcohol," I said. I thought briefly about my vow to study tonight but then figured that saving Starlocket mattered more than memorizing a list of presidents. Anyway, there would be plenty of time to study after Imbolc.

Killian threw back his head and laughed. "We have to get you up to speed," he said.

Even in our hungover state, we all gravitated toward the good time that Killian seemed to promise, and half an hour later we were sprawled in Bree's family room. I tried to sit next to Killian, determined to find out if he had passed my message on to Ciaran.

We were all making fun of Bree's awful CD of French pop music when the doorbell rang. When Bree came back to the family room she was followed by Sky Eventide, Alisa Soto, and Simon Bakehouse, who was also in Kithic. Jenna and Simon had recently started going out. Sky looked at Raven, who was leaning toward Killian, offering him a bite of a mini powdered doughnut.

Killian looked up at the newcomers and gave them a welcoming smile, licking powdered sugar off his lips. Bree, the good hostess, introduced him. Simon smiled politely.

"I remember Sky," Killian said in a silky voice, smiling into her eyes. Sky narrowed hers at him so they looked like slits of obsidian. She was dressed in formfitting black clothes, which made her moonlight-pale hair stand out in stark contrast. She turned to look at Raven, who had a bored expression on her face.

Simon sat next to Jenna, putting his hand on her knee as she smiled up at him. Across the room Matt looked like he'd just bitten a lemon. Alisa seemed uncomfortable and awkward and very young. She perched on the edge of the couch, and I wondered why she had come. This wasn't an official circle, after all.

"Well!" said Bree, artificially brightly. "Who needs something to drink? I have seltzer, juice, sodas, or I could make coffee or tea."

"How about a drop of whiskey?" Killian asked.

Only someone who knew Bree as well as I did could tell that she was disconcerted by his open request. "Sorry," she said. "The liquor cabinet's locked."

Killian laughed. "Lock or no lock—it doesn't matter to a witch."

Bree wasn't so easy to influence. "Sorry," she said again, with a touch more warning in her voice.

My glance flicked to Ethan, who looked relieved. Sharon reached up and rubbed the back of his neck under his long curls. He gave her a little smile, and she kissed him. I felt a renewed sense of warmth for both of them.

Only Bree was so irrevocably cool that she could say she didn't want to drink and not look like a Girl Scout. For the millionth time in my life, I admired her easy self-confidence.

We talked. We listened to music. We laughed at Killian's stories and told some of our own. Bree lit incense and candles when the sun went down. Her family room became a dimly lit, exotic, magickal place. Around dinnertime we ordered pizza and the people who needed to call their parents did. I checked in with Eileen to let her know where I'd be.

It was eight o'clock when I remembered again my intention to hit the books tonight. Today in school Mr. Alban had reminded us of an English composition that was due soon. My grades were slipping a little this semester—I had to get it together. I looked over at Killian, who seemed to be enjoying playing Sky and Raven off each other.

I sidled over to him and touched his shoulder. He leaned toward me, smiling, and I put my face close to his to speak privately. He slanted his head toward mine, and I felt so duplicitous, like a user.

"I was wondering if you had contacted our father yet," I said bluntly.

His dark eyes met mine, and I noticed for the first time that they tilted up at the corners ever so slightly, like mine. "Not yet," he said softly so only I could hear. "You're more eager to see him than I am."

I didn't know what to make of this and was still pondering my next step when Killian got up to get another can of soda. Damnation.

The clock was ticking even now, but still, I decided that pushing Killian was a bad idea. As Eoife had cautioned, I didn't want to make him suspicious of my motives—he was already cagey enough. Reluctantly I got to my feet. "Gotta go," I said, trying to remember where I had put my coat.

"No, no, little sister," Killian protested. "The night is young yet, and so are we." He laughed, and I felt my body tense in frustration.

"I better go study," I said, feeling like a failure again. At least my schoolwork was something I could control. There was no chance of ending up at a pub on the edge of town with my history book.

"Stay, love," Killian said coaxingly, and suddenly his voice was like a velvet ribbon wrapping around my wrists, keeping me there. Maybe my studying could wait. "Stay, and I'll show you some special magick."

Well, *that* was something worth checking out, at least. I sat back down.

He grinned in delight and gestured to the others. "Sit in a circle."

When we were in a circle, Killian again rubbed his hands together, as if he were a stage performer. Sky, sitting next to him, looked as if she would rather be eating glass. Killian cupped his hands and blew on them (I was sure that was just for effect) and then tossed a little ball of blue, crackly witch fire at Sky. Startled, she caught it in her cupped hands, and it transformed into a ball of glowing, pinkish light.

"Pass it!" Killian urged her.

With a little shrug Sky passed it to Robbie, next to her. Robbie looked fascinated, his face bright and a little scared, holding it in his hands. When Killian waved toward him, Robbie passed it to Bree, next to him. And around it went, this glowing ball of light. When it was my turn, I thought it felt like an electrified pom-pom. When it got back to Killian, he bounced it in one hand and looked at us.

"Now add to it," he said, once again tossing it lightly to Sky. She held the light for a moment, concentrating. It glowed a bit bigger and brighter, and she passed it to Robbie. Robbie did the same, with less perceptible results. Of this group only Killian, Sky, and I were blood witches. When we passed the light, it grew obviously bigger and brighter. When the others passed it, any change was less visible, but at the end of each circle round, the cumulative effect was definitely noticeable. And it became more sensitive to the increasing energy—after the fifth round Alisa passed it, and it jumped in size and brightness as it passed from her hands. She giggled nervously.

It was kind of a juvenile game, like hot potato, but it was also a beautiful, electric thing: making magick out of thin air. I could feel the magickal energy increasing, crackling around us, as if it were another presence in the room. Again and again we infused the light with our individual energies, watching as it changed color and brightness, depending on who held it. I felt filled with light, with energy, with magick, and it was exciting and satisfying in a way that nothing else could ever be.

The next time it landed in Killian's hands, he held it and then suddenly shot it straight at me. "Do something!" he commanded.

Without a moment to think, I opened my heart and my mind. I caught the witch fire lightly in my hands and spun it toward the ceiling, shaping it into a long blue stream of fire. Feeling magick flowing through me, surrounding me, I let the energy do what it wanted to, and I opened my hand out flat to release it. It bounced against the ceiling and then shattered like crystal, raining down on us in prickly, multicolored sparks.

"Oh my God," Jenna breathed, her eyes reflecting the pinpricks of light.

Flowers, I thought, and in the next instant the shower of sparks had changed into a gentle rain of real, petal-soft flowers, brushing gently against our faces. Tulips, daisies, poppies, anemones, all in summer-bright colors, landing as light as butterflies all around us. I smiled with pleasure at the beauty I had wrought. *Witch, witch,* I thought, claiming the title as my own.

Then I looked up. My friends' faces were a mixture of disbelief, amazement, and a little bit of fear, from Alisa. Even Robbie, who had been so concerned about my abuse of magick in New York, wore an expression of amazement and joy. Killian was smiling big at me, a familial smile that made me feel more connected to him. Sky was watching me with solemn silence, and I realized—too late, as always—that I had just committed another Wiccan faux pas or worse. Inwardly I groaned. There were so many rules! Things that felt so natural were bound and regulated.

My next thought was that I was supposed to get up extra early tomorrow to meet with Eoife before school. Hunter had relayed my report on last night's meeting, but I was supposed to check in with her in person.

I sighed and got to my feet.

8. Longing

Brother Colin, I have doubts that I have not been able to confess to good Father Benedict. My brother, I fear I am possessed by evil spirits. Since the night of Brother Thomas's healing, Nuala Riordan has haunted my waking moments and my dreams. Only during prayer does she not intrude upon my poor mind. I have mortified my flesh, I have prostrated myself before God, I have spent days and nights in prayer until I am half feverish.

My brother, if you have any hope for my immortal soul, please remember me in your prayers.

—Brother Sinestus Tor, to Colin, July 1768

When the alarm went off at six-thirty on Thursday morning, I felt like I was trapped in an unending nightmare. I pawed at the clock until the hideous noise stopped. Almost forty minutes later I awoke again, wondering if it was time to get up for school. Then I sat bolt upright. Eoife!

I threw some food at Dagda, scrambled into jeans and a

sweatshirt, quickly braided my hair, and was out of the house in less than twenty minutes. I was already late. My heart was pounding as I drove to Hunter's house, and not even the pinkish morning light soothed me. My life was out of control. Last night I'd gotten home after eleven. I had taken out my textbooks, then stared at them uncomprehendingly as my bed beckoned. Five minutes later I was asleep, with Dagda kneading the comforter next to me.

So for the last four days I hadn't done any homework, hadn't gotten enough sleep, hadn't gotten Ciaran to Widow's Vale. I was late for my meeting with Eoife, I wasn't checking in with her often enough, I'd made illegal magick. . . . What the hell was I doing?

I pulled up fast in front of the somewhat shabby little house that Hunter and Sky shared. The back deck that Cal had sabotaged had been rebuilt. There was an ugly ligustrum hedge in front that had been ignored for so many years that it was just a gnarled collection of half-leaved branches. My breath coming out in little puffs of smoke, I trotted up the walkway and rang their doorbell.

As I did, it occurred to me that I was at my ex-boyfriend's house at seven-thirty in the morning, looking like total hell. True, I had broken up with him, and for very good reasons, but that didn't mean I had to make him glad about it when he saw me by looking like a wreck.

Eoife opened the door, her small face solemn as she looked at me, and I wondered if Sky had mentioned the sparks-and-flowers incident of the night before.

"Sorry I'm late," I said. Without thinking I cast my senses through the house and discovered that Sky was asleep upstairs but Hunter wasn't in the house. Good. A reprieve.

"Do you always do that?" Eoife said as I followed her into the kitchen in back.

"Do what?" I took off my coat as Eoife poured boiling water into a waiting teapot.

"Cast your senses." She brought the teapot to the table, and smoky plumes of fragrance swirled above us. I inhaled deeply, enjoying the scent.

"Um . . ." I tried to think. "Yes, I guess so. I don't really think about it. But if I feel like I need to know what's going on, who's around, that kind of thing, then yeah, I guess I usually cast my senses."

She poured tea into two delicate cups with saucers. "Who taught you how to do that?"

"No one. It just came to me." I circled my left hand over my tea, widdershins, and thought, Cool the fire. Now the tea was the perfect temperature, and I took a long sip. Ahhh.

Frowning, not angrily but as if perplexed, Eoife looked at me from across the table. "You cooled your tea."

"Uh-huh. It's great. Thanks for making it." Another big swallow, hoping this tea had caffeine in it. I couldn't tell.

"Morgan—" Eoife began, but then shook her head. "Never mind."

I took a packet of Pop-Tarts out of my backpack and opened it. They're better toasted but perfectly edible cold if necessary. I offered one to Eoife and thought I detected a faint shudder as she refused.

Holding her teacup with both hands, Eoife said, "I'm sorry to tell you, Morgan, that Suzanna Mearis is still in a coma."

I looked at Eoife, and sudden guilt crashed down on me.

The truth was, I had barely thought of Suzanna in the last couple of days. I had been there to see her fall, I had witnessed the taibhs, I knew that her coven was destined for destruction, yet I had spent the last two days partying and abusing my power. What kind of a witch was I? "Has anything else happened?"

"Not as of this morning, thank the Goddess." She put down her cup and gazed at me. "Has Killian spoken to Ciaran?"

"Not yet," I admitted. "He said I'm more eager to see Ciaran than he is. I guess Ciaran's angry at him, and Killian wants to delay having to deal with it." I looked up at Eoife's chestnut-colored eyes, remembering again Suzanna's warm house and serene expression. "I feel like I should press harder," I admitted. "I know that you said not to make Killian suspicious, but Imbolc is getting closer and closer. Maybe if I told Killian I was desperate to meet my father again . . ."

I felt tension tightening Eoife's slight body. "No, Morgan," she said, leaning over the table. Her eyes burned in her porcelain face. "We have to tread cautiously. I know that this is difficult, but we mustn't destroy the mission by acting in haste."

I nodded slowly and looked deep into my teacup. "Okay," I murmured. "I'll keep working. Ciaran will come here, and I'll get information out of him."

Eoife sat back in her chair, her eyes still on me. "I'm sorry," she said again. "You make it easy to forget that you're young and uninitiated."

"I can do this," I said firmly, pushing aside my tea. Looking vaguely sympathetic, Eoife nodded back at me, and I picked up my coat and left.

* * *

School seemed more surreal than usual that morning since I had just come from a meeting with Eoife. I felt schizophrenic: high school student by day, undercover ICOW agent by night. In first period I had barely sat down when my American history teacher, Mr. Powell, pulled out an ominous sheaf of papers.

"As I mentioned last Friday," he said, starting to hand them out, "this is a test on what we've learned since the winter holidays."

I stared at him in horror, then mentally said every bad word I could think of. Tara Williams handed the pile of papers back to me, and I numbly took one and passed the rest to Jeff Goldstein. Just this morning I had worried about my life being out of control. Here was the proof. My grades had been slipping, and in three months I had gone from being a straight-A student to a straight-B student with maybe even a couple of Cs, which my parents were going to freak about. Now I was about to get a big, fat F on this test.

Unless . . .

Unless. I thought about Killian, about his charm, his skill, the easy comfort with which he did things. Life had not come pleasantly for my half brother, but he'd gone a long way to making it easier and more fun. What would he do in this situation?

I looked up at Mr. Powell. All it would take was a simple spell that would make Mr. Powell forget he'd intended to give us this test. Or to think this one was the wrong test, and he'd bring another tomorrow. Or to think we were supposed to have the test next week.

I bit my lip. What was I thinking? This was exactly what Hunter always talked about: making the wrong decision, making the decision that benefits only yourself, making the decision that doesn't take other people into account. He always said that was why the council had introduced regulations and guidelines back in the early 1800s. Because it's so easy to make the wrong small decision. And once you do, it's even easier to make the wrong big decision. And then, boom. You're part of the darkness.

I made choices every day, all day long. I needed to be more aware of all of them, needed to consciously try to make the right decision, a decision for good. I resigned myself to the fact that the only thing I would get right on this test was my own name.

When Killian wasn't waiting for me after school, I felt relief as well as disappointment. I could try sending him a witch message, I knew—but maybe that would make him suspicious. After all, we had seen each other almost every day this week. Would I seem too clingy if I called him today, too?

"Want to come hang out?" Bree asked as I walked toward Das Boot. "Robbie and I are going to my house for a while."

"Thanks," I said. "But I've been letting a lot of things slide. I better get home and crank."

"Okay. See you later."

I started my car and turned the heater up. I wondered where Bree and Robbie were in their relationship and how it was going. Although I had been seeing all my friends every day this week, I felt oddly disconnected from them. Being with Killian had meant only fun and magick. Unfortunately for my mission, it hadn't meant really talking to each other, sharing our feelings, or feeling closer.

Okay. Now I was all touchy-feely. This was getting me nowhere. I had to focus: concentrate on getting Killian to call Ciaran, getting closer to both of them, saving Starlocket.

There wasn't any time to think about my own problems. And probably, I thought as my heart sank into my stomach, that was a good thing.

When I got home, I cleaned the kitchen, loaded the dishwasher for the first time since my parents had left, fed Dagda and cleaned his litter box, and called Aunt Eileen.

"Yep, everything's fine," I told her, trying to sound like that was true. "No—no coed sleepovers. At least not yet. Ha ha." After we hung up, I headed upstairs to my room and determinedly sat down at my desk. I would study for a while, then send a witch message to Killian, asking him about Ciaran.

I started with American history, reviewing chapters and making notes. I hoped that I could undo some of the damage of today's test with extra credit. Dagda came and settled himself on my desk right under the heat of the lamp.

"You have it good," I told him. "No school, no parents, no choices between good and evil. No history tests."

Ugh. If only I could simply do a tàth meànma brach with Mr. Powell and just absorb all his knowledge. Then I could ace this class.

A couple of hours later I ate an apple with peanut butter for dinner and got ready to send a witch message to Killian. I was just calming my thoughts to do it when my senses tingled: Hunter was coming up the walk. I still seemed to be able to pick up on his vibrations more easily than I could almost anyone else's.

It occurred to me that the last time I saw him, I'd been throwing up my guts. So I felt really lovely and feminine, waiting for him to come to the door. At least this time my face was clean.

"Hi," I said as he stepped onto the porch.

"Hi." His green eyes swept me from head to foot. "How are you feeling?"

"Fine. Thanks for your help the other night," I said, not looking at him.

"You're welcome," he said, just as coolly. "I'm here to receive your report. Can we go inside?"

What report? I wondered. I'd given my report to Eoife this morning. Had he not heard it from her? Or was there some other reason he wanted to come over? Puzzled, I frowned at him for a second before realizing he'd asked me a question.

"No, you're not supposed to be in the house. Here, let's sit in Das Boot," I said, digging in my pocket for the keys. It was frigid inside my car, and the vinyl seats didn't help any. But I blasted the heater, and a few minutes later we were comfortable.

"You met with Eoife this morning?" he asked, taking off his gloves and shoving them in his pocket.

"Yes. Is Suzanna Mearis still in a coma?"

He shook his head. "They did healing spells all day, and she woke up a little while ago."

I sighed in relief. "Thank the Goddess."

"Yes." Hunter nodded somberly, then turned his green eyes back to mine. "So tell me about Killian."

I shrugged. "I saw him yesterday at Bree's. Practically everyone from Kithic was there. I asked him if he had contacted Ciaran, and he said he hadn't. Didn't Eoife tell you this?"

Hunter frowned, and I got it: he was here because he had an excuse to be here, with me. Oh, Hunter, I thought longingly.

"Anyway," I said, looking at my hands, "I was about to send him a witch message, asking to get together."

"He's unbelievably slippery," Hunter said, almost to himself.

"Excuse me?"

"He gets out of everything, like an eel," Hunter went on. "He got out of New York before the ritual, he got off scot-free the night you were sick. He careens through life, having a good time and not worrying about anyone else."

"I think that's a little harsh," I said. "Killian's—incredibly fun. He's irresponsible, but I don't think he's hurtful. There's no reason to think he's deliberately keeping Ciaran from meeting me."

Hunter looked at me, and all at once I remembered other times sitting in my car, with our hands all over each other and our mouths joined fiercely. I swallowed and looked away.

"Give up the mission," Hunter said quietly.

"No. I'm getting it done."

"I don't think anyone can do it. It's too dangerous. I think Starlocket needs to disband and get out of town."

"Why don't they?" I asked.

He sighed. "Covens never do. When they're in danger, they stay together, no matter what. A coven never splits up if they can help it. Almost never." He paused, and I knew he was thinking about his parents. "Most covens feel they're less at risk if they stay together—the dark wave can't divide and conquer them."

Thinking about what Starlocket was facing, I once again felt the fear that I was sickeningly inadequate for this job. But somehow Hunter thinking that, too, was enough to make me go forward.

"We still have nine days. This could still work," I said.

Hunter shook his head, looking out the car window at the darkness. "Want to go have something to eat?" he surprised me by saying.

"I already ate. I've been studying all afternoon, trying to get caught up."

"Deities? Correspondences? Basic forms of spellcraft?"

"Uh, American history. For school."

Hunter nodded and looked away, and I felt that once again I had disappointed him somehow. Sometimes it seemed like everything I did was wrong.

"I flunked a test today, so I'm trying to catch up." Hoping to make Hunter smile, I said, "I'm so tempted to do a tàth meànma on my teacher so I wouldn't have to study the rest of the year."

His eyes flicked to me. "Morgan. Doing a tàth meànma with a regular human would likely leave that person a drooling vegetable."

"I was just kid—"

"Rules about things like that exist for a reason," he went on. "Witches have been using magick for thousands of years. Witches far more experienced than you have created these guidelines to benefit everyone. They saw what could happen if magick was unchecked."

"I was just *kidding*," I said stiffly. Sometimes Hunter seemed so inflexible and humorless. He wasn't, I knew, but he definitely *seemed* that way sometimes.

"Things are very clear for you, aren't they?" I asked almost wistfully. "Decisions seem clear, the right path is in front of you, you don't have to agonize over what's right or wrong."

He was silent for a few minutes. I cracked a window so we wouldn't die of carbon monoxide poisoning. "Is that how I seem to you?" he asked softly, his words barely reaching me.

I nodded.

"It isn't true." His words were like velvety leaves, falling between us in the darkness. "Sometimes nothing is clear. Sometimes there is no right path, no correct decision. Sometimes I absolutely want what I shouldn't have and do what I shouldn't do. Sometimes I want to reach out, grab power from the air, and bend everything around me to my will." He gave a slight smile as I reacted to his words. "So far I haven't," he said more lightly. "Most of the time I do all right. But not always, and not without a struggle."

I'd never known this about him, and of course it made me fall even more in love with him than I already had. He had vulnerabilities. He wasn't perfect. Oh, Goddess, I wanted him so much.

"That's what magick is," he said. "Many choices, through your lifetime. How you make them determines who you are. And who you are determines how you make them."

Wicca is full of pithy sayings like that. I was tempted to write them all down in a book and watch it become a best-seller. *Chicken Soup for the Witch's Soul.*

But I knew what he meant. I got it. I rubbed my hands down my jeans. "I'll go call Killian."

"All right. Be careful. Call me if you need me. Don't do anything that feels unsafe."

I smiled wanly. "Yes, Dad."

In a move so fast I didn't see it, Hunter was across the seat, his arm around my back, holding me against him, hard. As I gasped in surprise, he slanted his mouth across mine and kissed me with a hunger and an urgency that rocked me to the core. *Yes, yes, yes.* Just as suddenly he pulled back, leaving me wide-eyed and breathing fast and awash in a desire so strong, I didn't know what to do with it.

"I'm not your dad," he said, looking at me. Then he opened his door and got out. Agape, I watched him head to his own car, his long wool coat billowing around his legs like a cape. I was shaking, and my arms felt empty because he wasn't in them.

9.
True Name

I am sorry for the delay in answering your last two letters. I have been ill. The summer grass sickness felled our community, and we have lost both Brother Sean and Brother Paul Marcus, God have mercy on their souls.

Myself, I owe my sad life to Nuala, who nursed me back from death not once but several times. In a babe's weak voice I bid that pawn of the devil to be gone. She laughed, her voice like a mountain stream. Surely you'll not think me evil, said she. Truly, we in Belwicket do more good than you, holed up in your abbey of gloom.

Through my delirium I insisted she did the devil's work. She bent close to me, so that her black hair fell across my chest. In a whisper she told me, "We do no work but that which should be done. My ancestors were gathering knowledge while your people were still fighting the Crusades."

I felt as if I were drowning. Today my head is clearer, and I do not know whether that interview took place. Remember me in your prayers, Brother Colin, I beg you.

—Brother Sinestus Tor, to Colin, August 1768

In American history I got a forty-seven on my test. I had never flunked a test before in my life, and my stomach clenched in a knot of embarrassment.

"Morgan, can you see me after class, please?" said Mr. Powell.

I nodded, my face flushing.

After class I waited until the other kids had left. Mr. Powell looked up at me, his wide gray eyes thoughtful behind gold-wire glasses. "What happened with this test?" he jumped in with no preamble.

"I forgot about it," I admitted.

He looked perplexed. "But even if you forgot, you should have known enough to squeak by with a D. This test shows that you've learned virtually nothing since the winter holidays. I don't get it."

I was so hating this. "I just . . . I've just had a lot going on."

Once again he waited. I'd always liked Mr. Powell, even though I couldn't stand American history. I felt he always tried to make it interesting.

"Morgan, I'll be frank with you." I hate it when teachers say that. "You've always been an excellent student. But the other teachers and I have noticed a significant drop in your grades this past quarter." He paused, as if waiting for me to explain. I didn't know what to say. "Morgan, I've heard . . . rumors."

I blinked. "Rumors? About what?"

"About Wicca. Students having witchcraft circles, performing rites." He looked as uncomfortable as I felt. How in the world had he heard about that? Then I remembered the kids who had come to one or two of Cal's first circles. They'd left—it wasn't for them. I guessed they'd been talking about it.

"Do you know anything about it?" he pressed.

I felt like he was asking if I had ever been a member of the Communist Party, if I was gay, if I was Jewish. "Um, well, I practice Wicca." Morgan takes a stand.

Mr. Powell looked nonplussed for a moment, then tapped his fingers on his desk, thinking. Finally he said, "Is this interfering in your schoolwork?"

"Yes," I almost whispered. Far from being surreal, I was smack-dab in the middle of harsh reality. I was going to flunk my junior year if I didn't get my act together.

"What are you going to do about it?" he asked.

"Study more?"

"Will that be enough?"

"Do extra credit?" I offered hopefully.

"Let me think about it." He shut his notebook, no longer seeming approachable.

"I'm sorry," I said, and he looked back at me.

"Morgan, you're only seventeen. You're extremely bright. You could do anything you want with your life. Don't screw up this young." He turned and walked out of the room, as if he was personally hurt by my poor grade. I felt awful. I was being slowly crushed by pressure from all sides. I just had to get through and do the best I could do. The problem was, that probably wouldn't be good enough. For anyone.

"Morgan!" Killian was waiting for me on his usual bench. But as I started toward him, I heard Mary K.'s voice behind me. My heart clutched suddenly—I didn't want them to meet. Quickly I turned my back to Killian and went to meet my sister.

"I didn't see you this morning." She grinned. "Let me guess. You're having a hard time getting up in the morning."

"You know me too well. How are things at Jaycee's?"

My sister's face clouded. "It's fine," she said unconvincingly. "Jaycee's got a new friend—you know her. Alisa Soto. And a new boyfriend—Michael Pulaski."

I wasn't sure, but I thought Michael was a sophomore. "She sounds busy."

"Yeah." Mary K. shook her head. "I guess I'm not really used to sharing Jaycee. And Alisa's into Wicca, and I don't want Jaycee to get into it." This said with an apologetic glance. I knew she hated my involvement with Wicca. "And it's hard to watch her being all happy and lovey-dovey with Michael after—"

"Hmmm," I said. "Yeah. I can see how that would bother you. Are you going to tell Jaycee how you feel about these things?"

"No. It wouldn't do any good, and it'd just make me look weird and clingy. Anyway. We're going to the mall tonight 'cause it's Friday. Alisa isn't going, and Michael has hockey practice."

"Good. You and Jaycee have a good time, then. And call me tomorrow, okay? Since I won't see you at school."

She nodded. "Okay. Thanks." She gave me one of her quick, sweet smiles, and I felt a rush of love for her. My sister.

After Mary K. had rejoined her friends, I walked over to Killian. Raven was practically in his lap. I wondered meanly how she avoided getting pneumonia, showing as much skin as she did. As I walked up, other members of Kithic drifted toward us.

"Hey!" Killian greeted me. "I found something I wanted to show you all. Do we have enough cars?"

And just that easily we were all swept into the Killian tide. Fifteen minutes later I realized we were almost to the old Methodist cemetery where our original coven, Cirrus, had first made magick. Where Cal and Hunter had had a showdown and I had put a holding spell on Hunter that he was probably still pissed about. What had Killian found here?

"We've been here before," Matt told him as we gathered at the edge of the property.

"You have? Then you know about the power sink?" Killian looked disappointed.

"What power sink?" I asked, and he perked up and began to lead us through the overgrown brush to the actual graveyard.

"You know about power leys?" he asked. At our blank faces, he went on. "All around the earth, like strings wrapped around a ball, there are ancient lines of power that were created when the world was made. If a witch stands on one, works magick on one, their magick will be enhanced, more powerful. Anytime two or more of these leys intersect, the inherent power is even greater. Right in this cemetery is a huge power sink, probably five or more lines crossed together."

It was somehow demoralizing that my party-guy, irresponsible, devil-may-care half brother was so much more knowledgeable than I was. Then we were standing in front of the stone sarcophagus that Cirrus had used as an altar on Samhain. The marker read Jacob Henry Moore, 1845–1871.

"Right here!" Killian said enthusiastically. "This is an incredible power sink."

Bree met my eyes, and the other Kithic members were quiet. Cal had brought us here several times. Obviously he'd been aware it was a power sink and had used it to his advantage. And none of us had known.

It occurred to me that of course Hunter knew about it also. He must have felt it when he was here with Cal. The power sink might even be the reason my holding spells had worked so well when I'd used them to stop Hunter and Cal from fighting. But Hunter hadn't told me.

"Is a power sink important?" Bree asked.

"Oh, yes," said Killian. "It's like turbocharging your magick—for both good and bad. I mean, sometimes magick shouldn't be turbocharged. Know what I mean?"

"No," Robbie said.

"I mean, some spells need to be gentle and shallow," Killian explained.

While he was talking, I felt paranoia creeping into my veins. Quickly I cast my senses out strongly, sweeping the area for any kind of danger, anything out of the ordinary. Killian looked at me, his brows knit together, but I didn't stop until I was sure there was nothing unusual going on. Then I met his gaze calmly, and he cocked his head to the side.

"Watch this," he said, and held out his left arm. He wore a thick suede glove on his hand and pulled the heavy wool tweed of his coat over his wrist. Then he opened his mouth and began to sing into the setting afternoon light. It was an odd, unholy song, in a voice nothing like his own. It sounded inhuman but also frighteningly, hauntingly beautiful. The notes rose and fell and waxed and waned, and all the time my half brother, Ciaran's son, watched the sky. I realized he was repeating the song over again, and we all started watching the sky also.

Slowly, in the deepening twilight, I became aware of a large bird wheeling above us, dropping down toward us in reluctant spirals of grace.

"Uh-oh," Ethan breathed, and Sharon moved closer to him.

I could now see that the bird was a large red-tailed hawk, big enough to pick up a small dog in its talons. It dipped and swayed above us, descending ever slower as if being reeled in on a kite string.

"What are you doing?" I whispered.

"I know its true name," Killian said. "It can't resist me."

We all stepped back as the large, powerful predator dropped the last eight feet, wings beating, to land on Killian's arm. I couldn't breathe. This wasn't a zoo bird, wings clipped so it couldn't fly. This was a raw piece of nature, a killing machine, with eyes the color of liquid gold and a beak designed for ripping open rabbits' stomachs like silk. Its talons gripped Killian's coat sleeve, but if it hurt, he didn't show it.

"So beautiful," Jenna whispered, looking mesmerized.

The bird was clearly nervous and afraid, not comprehending why it was here, so against its will, against its nature. I could smell the fear coming off it, an acrid fragrance overlaid by anger and humiliation.

"That is one fine bird," Ethan said in awe.

"Incredible," said Bree.

"Let it go," I said with clenched teeth. "Let it go *now*."

Killian looked at me in surprise—the killjoy—then spoke some words. Instantly, as if released from a prison, the hawk took off. Its powerful wings beat the air with a sound like a helicopter's rotors. Within seconds it was a dark speck in the sky, leaving us behind.

"Well," Killian began.

"It hated being here," I said impatiently. "It *hated* it. It was afraid."

Killian looked intrigued. "How do you know?"

"I felt it!" I said. "Just like you must have."

"How did you do that?" Raven asked, interrupting us.

Killian turned to her, as if he had forgotten his audience. "I know its true name. The song I sang was its true name, the name that it was born with. Everything has a true name that's irrevocable and individual and unmistakable. If you know something's true name, you have power over it."

"Is a true name like a coven name?" Matt asked.

Shaking his head, Killian said, "No. No one can give something else its true name. It's part of the thing or the person, like eye color or skin color or the size of your hands. You're born with it, you die with it."

"Do you have a true name?" Raven asked.

He laughed, showing the smooth column of his neck. "Of course. Blood witches learn their true name during initiation. Everything has one, every person, every rock, every tree, every fish or bird or mammal. Crystals, metals—anything natural. They all have a true name. And if you know it, you own them."

I watched Killian intently. *Own* them? There was a difference between owning a living being versus a crystal or even a plant. I wondered what my true name was. A chill went down my spine as I considered what might happen if somebody else were to know it. If there was one thing I had learned over the past few months, it was that there were plenty of people out there who would love to be able to *own* me and my power.

"Does anyone else know your true name?" Robbie asked Killian. "Like your parents?"

"Oh, Goddess, no!" Killian looked appalled at the thought. "It gives someone power over you if they know your true name."

"You don't want your parents to know?" Robbie asked.

"And give them power over me? Never. I'd rather be dead." All his humor was gone, and his face was closed and set. He glanced at the empty, darkening sky. "It's getting late. We'd better go."

As we walked back to the cars, I thought about what Killian had just done. It had been beautiful; beautiful, painful magick. He had forced a living thing to act against its nature, and he had done it lightly, capriciously, and solely to impress. He had broken about a hundred council rules with this one stunt. If every witch were like this, it would be a disaster. I began to comprehend the role the council played in the order of witches.

I was almost to Das Boot when Killian took my arm gently. He leaned close to whisper in my ear: "Speaking of parents . . . I heard from Da. He's coming to see us."

10. Blood Ties

Brother Colin, my battles are usually of the spirit, but today I had one of the flesh. On the road home from Atherton to Barra Head, I saw three roadside bandits set upon Nuala Riordan.

I commanded them to unhand her, and two of them immediately set upon me. God forgive me, Brother Colin, but it was as if I were a lad once more, wrestling with you and Derwin. You'll remember that I always trounced you both at wrestling, and I trounced both those sorry louts today. As for the third, he fell into some sort of fit; with no warning he fell to the ground, writhing in pain. At last he fainted, and Nuala and I left with all haste.

Thanks be to God, she was unharmed. When I suggested that perhaps she should not leave the village without her husband, she looked at me oddly. Then boldly she told me she had no husband, nor a lover, either.

My cheeks burned at her frankness, Brother Colin, I admit it. Then, as softly as a dove's wing, she said my name—Sinestus—and it was as if her very voice were weaving a spell around me. I left her as quickly as I could, for to speak truth, I feared the temptation of sin.

It is time for vespers, Brother Colin, and then Brother Edmond is taking the post. I must finish this letter another time.

—Brother Sinestus Tor, to Colin, September 1768

"Well, I'm still fine," I told Aunt Eileen the next day. So far. I checked her name off my list of phone calls.

"Are you sure?" she asked. "Why don't you come spend the weekend here?"

"Oh, that's okay," I said. "I'm just going to stay home and study. I need to pull up some grades."

"You? Pull them up to what? What's past an A?"

I laughed nervously. We chatted a few more minutes, then hung up.

Next I called Mary K. at Jaycee's. It turned out that Jaycee's parents were taking the girls skiing for the weekend. I felt relief. I'd spent most of the night lying awake, dreading Ciaran's arrival. I wanted Mary K. away from here—I didn't want her associated with whatever happened between me and my blood father. I told her to be careful and to not break her leg and asked if she needed money, which she didn't. She was a chronic baby-sitter and consequently as rich as Midas.

"Take care," I told her. "Use your good manners."

She laughed at my Mom imitation.

Next on my phone list was Hunter. "I haven't heard from Killian yet," I reported. "I don't know when Ciaran's coming in."

"All right. Listen, I just got a cell phone. Write down this number."

I did.

"Now I need you to come to my house. Eoife's here, and we need to talk about plans and also teach you some spells you'll need to deal with Ciaran."

I sighed. So much for hitting the books today. "Okay," I said. "I'll be there soon."

"Try to hurry."

"All right." We said our good-byes, and I went to take a shower.

Hunter let me in half an hour later. When I saw Eoife perched on the couch in the living room, my mood darkened. She looked paler, more fragile than the last time I had seen her, as if she were carrying a heavier weight. She gave me a faint smile.

"So you were successful," she told me.

"Well, Killian says he's coming. We'll have to see if he does or not," I said.

"He'll come," said Hunter, already pouring tea. "Now, tell us again everything Killian has told you."

I did. I drank my tea, feeling its warmth slide down my throat, soothing me from the inside out. I told them about Killian finding the power sink at the cemetery and met Hunter's eyes. His expression betrayed nothing. I told them any snippets of conversation I had remembered, anything he had mentioned about his family. I felt disloyal to Killian, doing this, yet that had been the plan. That was what I had signed up for.

"Anything else?" Hunter said, his eyes on me.

I thought about the hawk spell and closed my mind to Hunter. I didn't even know why, except I didn't want to get

Killian in trouble. He didn't seem evil to me—just irresponsible. I wondered if he even understood the abuses that knowing something's true name might lead to. When I looked up, Eoife's eyes seemed to look right through me, and I prayed I didn't blush. I wasn't fooling either one of them. Was I already failing the inherent test in all this, my choosing good over evil not just sometimes, but every time? I felt so inadequate.

Hunter expelled his breath and sat back in his chair. He ran long fingers through his short blond hair, and to me it seemed like he only became more attractive every time I saw him. The bastard.

"Right," said Eoife, sitting up straighter. "So let's talk about Starlocket. Suzanna Mearis has come out of her coma but has paralysis on her left side. They're continuing to work healing spells but since they don't know exactly what spell Amyranth used against her, they haven't been successful. In the meantime smaller things continue to happen: Rina O'Fallon's car lost its steering, and she had an accident. Someone's cat was found dead of no apparent cause. Someone's winter garden wilted overnight in its cold frame."

I digested this silently.

"The noose is closing," Hunter murmured.

"Why can't they disband?" I asked, wanting it clarified.

"It's traditional not to, in times of trouble," Eoife said, her eyes sad. "The bond between coven members is considered unbreakable. Only in very rare, extraordinary circumstances do members separate during dangerous times." Her glance flicked toward Hunter, and I remembered again that his parents had fled along with the rest of their coven before it was destroyed by a dark wave. I wondered what that extraordinary circumstance had been, but Hunter's face gave no clue.

I felt that if I were in Starlocket, I'd be in Tennessee by now.

"They're determined to fight evil in all its forms," Eoife added. "But I did tell them that we're still working to infiltrate Amyranth, and they were much cheered by this news."

I looked at her blankly, then gulped when I realized that their only hope was me. If something happened to Alyce and Starlocket because I wasn't strong enough, good enough, how could I ever live with myself? Assuming I survived.

"Anyway," said Hunter briskly, "we need to teach you some sigils of concealment and more wards of protection."

"Yes," Eoife began, but then we were distracted by Sky's angry voice coming from the kitchen.

"Dammit, that's not what I meant, and you know it!" she was practically shouting.

"Who's here?" I asked. I hadn't picked up on anyone else's presence.

Hunter shook his head. "No one. She must be on the phone."

"Anyway, Morgan," Eoife went on, "one of the first things I want to teach you is a simple concealment spell. It doesn't literally make you invisible, of course, but most people, animals, and even witches won't notice you're there."

I nodded. "Like a you-see-me-not spell."

Eoife looked startled. "You do this already?"

"Um, only occasionally," I answered, wondering if I had just stepped on more Wiccan toes. "You know, if I don't . . . uh, want to be seen."

Eoife shot Hunter a glance, and he sort of threw up his hands, as if I were an unhousebroken dog he'd tried his best with.

"Raven, I'm talking about last night!" Sky interrupted us loudly.

We all felt embarrassed to be hearing this conversation. Then Eoife shook her head and focused again.

"This spell should get you into and out of most situations," she said. "If Ciaran knows you quite well, if he's familiar with your vibrations and your aura, he may be able to pick up on it, but not right away."

"He knows some of that, if not all," I said, thinking back to New York. He'd tried to steal my magick, so yeah, he probably knew my aura.

"We'll have to do the best we can," Eoife said. "Ciaran is quite adept at knowing one intimately, only to use that knowledge to destroy. He enjoys destruction in and of itself, which is why he's so dangerous. He enjoys the act itself, not just the dividends. He is the opposite of a creator."

I hated hearing this about Ciaran but knew immediately it was true. What had happened in his life to make him that way? How much of his legacy had he passed on to me, to Killian, to his other children? Knowing he was evil the way I did, how could I still remember our odd connection with longing? What did that say about me?

Eoife moved to sit cross-legged in front of the fire crackling in Hunter's fireplace. Gesturing to me to sit across from her, she said, "We'll bolster this with other spells of protection and attack. With your inherent strength, I feel it will work. If you learn it perfectly."

Sitting across from Eoife on the floor, I tried to clear my mind and relax my breathing. I could still hear Sky in the kitchen, her voice rising and falling in anger. I tried to block it out. Hunter stayed where he was, in his chair, but I felt his eyes on me unwaveringly.

"We'll start with the words," said Eoife, starting to murmur them.

Leaning closer, I let my mind expand to envelop the softly spoken words. I loved spellcraft. There were so many different kinds: ones using crystals, oils, incenses, herbs. Ones using only words, ones combining words and gestures, ones made only within a circle and some you could make anywhere. This one had three parts: words, runes written in the air, and the casting of a glamor.

Ten minutes later I had the words and runes down pat and felt confident I would remember them. The casting of a glamour I would have to work on. It was odd, but unlike school learning, which could sometimes go in me like a stone sinking in water, never to be seen again—magick seemed quite different. I had never forgotten a spell. Once learned, it seemed part of the fabric of my being, another colored thread that made up the complete Morgan.

I almost jumped when Sky raised her voice again.

"No!" she shouted. "That's not what I'm saying. You're twisting my words."

I really didn't want to hear any more and had stood up to ask if we could go work in the circle room, when Sky stalked out of the kitchen, her black eyes shooting sparks of anger. She saw us sitting there, and her gaze lasered in on me.

"He's *your* brother," she said acidly. "You brought him here. He's a total bastard, and Raven's thick enough not to see it. But she should know better—after all, he's Woodbane." This last was spit at me, and I felt the blood drain from my face as she grabbed her black leather jacket and slammed out of the house. Outside I heard the roar of Sky's car as she peeled out, brakes squealing.

It was true: I *had* brought Killian here, and Raven *was* making a fool of herself over him, with his enthusiastic help. But I had brought him here at the council's wishes and for the greater good. I sat there feeling mortified, not knowing what to say. Hunter looked tight-lipped and withdrawn, but Eoife was calm as she arranged the tea things on their tray.

"This is all part of life, my dear," she said in her soft Scottish accent. "Even pain and embarrassment are part of it."

With a heavy sigh Hunter reached over and patted my knee. "Sky's just really angry. Not every Woodbane is evil," he said. "Your mother wasn't. Belwicket wasn't. I'm half Woodbane. There are many, many good Woodbanes out there."

"But not Killian, right?" I asked somberly. "And not Ciaran."

Neither Hunter nor Eoife spoke, and silently I reached for my coat and let myself out of that house. Once again my heritage was catching up to me.

11. Shades of Gray

I thank you for trying to intercede on my behalf, but it has been decided, Brother Colin. I have been remanded to the abbey at Habenstadt, in Prussia. I expected such action to be taken against me once I confessed my many sinful thoughts to Father Benedict. And how can I question the fairness, the wisdom of such a judgment? There, away from the source of my temptation, among the contemplatives, perhaps God will show me a path through my tortured mind. As for Nuala, she has disappeared. I pray that God watches over her.

—Brother Sinestus Tor, to Colin, April 1769

That night, at Bree's house, Raven didn't show for the circle.

I'd arrived on time, and I was wearing cargo pants and a soft, thin sweater. After I'd gotten home from Hunter's, I'd felt depressed and confused, so I had cleaned the kitchen, done some laundry, scooped Dagda's box, and promised myself to try not to look so scruffy all the time.

After Bree opened the door, the first person I saw was

Sky. I was still stinging from her Woodbane comment but at the same time knew she was in love with Raven and getting burned and was not in a good frame of mind.

"I think we're all here," Hunter said. His voice sounded both rough and melodious, and for no good reason I suddenly remembered how his voice sounded in my ear, talking to me when we were making out, hearing his breath coming hard and fast because of what we were doing. I felt myself blush and turned away from him, taking a long time to dump my coat on the pile in the hallway.

"Let's go into the den," Bree said. "It's more comfy in there."

"Actually," Hunter said, "I checked it out and it's full of electronics and furniture. Do you have someplace more bare?"

Which is how we ended up sitting in a chalk circle on the flagstones at one end of her enclosed pool. Above us we could see the stars, wavering and dim through the glass enclosure. The furniture had been stacked and covered; the water was still and dark. The vibrations were very different here, surrounded by water and stone and glass.

"While we wait to see if Raven's coming," said Hunter, "let's go around the circle and get a quick rundown of what you've been up to, what you've been studying, any questions you have, and so on. We should be preparing for Imbolc, also. It's a time to think about new beginnings." He nodded to Matt, who was sitting on his right.

Matt was starting to look more like himself after weeks and weeks of looking both odd and somewhat disheveled. Tonight he was wearing a dark red velour sweatshirt and black cords, and his thick black hair was neatly cut and brushed smoothly back. "I'm okay. I've been doing some general studying of correspondences—especially how to work with crystals."

"Good," said Hunter. "Next?"

Thalia sat up straighter. I didn't know Thalia all that well; like Alisa, she had been part of the original Kithic coven, led by Sky, before they had absorbed the six of us who had been in the Cirrus coven, originally led by Cal. "I've been crazed with a science project. Other than that I've been reading a book about candle-burning rituals. It's really interesting."

"I'm still doing a lot with the tarot," said Bree. "I'm really loving it. Every time I do a reading, it's like a therapy session. I have to sit and really think about what the cards said and how it applies to my life."

Robbie was next. "My dad lost his job. Again. Mom's threatening to kick him out. Again. He'll get another job, Mom will get off his back, everything will be back to normal. Again. It's a little stressful, but I'm used to it. In terms of Wicca, I've been reading Ellis Hindworth's *Basic History of the White Art.*"

"That's a good book," said Hunter. "I hope things quiet down for you at home."

Sharon, Ethan, and Jenna all checked in. Simon Bakehouse, between Jenna and me, said he'd been studying Celtic deities.

I thought about how ironic it was that Amyranth was planning to destroy Starlocket at Imbolc, which is supposed to be a time of rebirth. It seemed especially horrible. I felt a twinge of panic at the weight of my responsiblity. When it was my turn to speak, I cleared my throat. "I've been studying a bunch of different stuff—history and spells and the basics of spellcraft. I'm having a hard time in school. And my parents are against Wicca."

Alisa Soto was next. Most of us were seventeen and eighteen, and so she, at fifteen, seemed very young. "My dad is against Wicca, too. He thinks it's some kind of weird cult. I don't get it. Two of my aunts practice Santeria, so he should accept alternative religions. I've been reading a biography of a woman who discovered Wicca and what it meant to her."

Last was Sky. She didn't look at any of us, and her voice was low and steady, almost expressionless. "I've been studying the medicinal uses of herbs. I'm thinking about going back to England for a while."

I looked at her in surprise, wondering if she wanted to leave because of how Raven was acting. Sky and I had never been close, but we had forged a mutually respectful relationship, and I would miss her if she left.

"Okay," said Hunter. He didn't look surprised. I figured that this must be something he and Sky had already discussed. Turning back to the circle, he held a hand out to each side. "I guess we can assume Raven's not coming, so let's stand up, join hands, close our eyes, and concentrate. Relax everything, release any pent-up energy, focus on your breathing, and open up to receive magick."

Now the twelve of us stood in a circle. Hunter and Bree had lit many candles, and they surrounded us, flickering with our movements. I was beneath stars, next to water, standing on stone, in a circle of magick, and I felt that quick, ecstatic fluttering in my chest that told me my body was open to receive what the Goddess wanted to give me.

Slowly we moved deasil around our central candle. Hunter started a basic power chant, one we'd used before. Our voices wove together like ribbons, like warm and cold ocean currents sliding into one. Our faces were lit by candles, by joy, by fellowship, by an unexpected yet required trust of each other. Our feet flew across the flagstones, our energy rose, and the magick came down and surrounded us, lifting our hearts, filling us with peace and excitement, making our hair crackle with static. During this time my worries about Ciaran, my dangerous mission, my fears all melted away. This was pure white magick, and it seemed a million miles away from the darkness and destruction that Ciaran represented.

I could have stayed in the circle all night, whirling, feeling the magick, feeling beautiful and strong and whole and safe. But gently, gently, Hunter brought it down, slowed our steps, smoothed the energy, and then we sank gently onto the stones again, our knees touching, our hands linked, our faces flushed and expectant.

"Everyone take a moment, close your eyes, and think of what you'll turn your energy toward," Hunter said softly. "What do you need help with, what are you ready to know, what are you able to give? Open your heart and let the answer come, and when you're finished, look up again."

My head drooped, and my eyes fluttered shut. There was a strong, pulsing cord of white magick inside me, there for the taking, there for me to use as I would. The answer came to me almost immediately. *Let me save Starlocket. Let me protect Alyce from harm.*

I straightened and opened my eyes to see Hunter looking at me intently. He blinked when I met his gaze and looked away. What had I seen in his eyes?

When everyone had looked up, we dropped our hands, and Hunter began the lesson.

"I want to talk about light and dark," he said, his English accent seeming elegant and precise. "Light and dark are, of course, two sides of the same coin. They make up everything we know in life. This concept has been more readily described as the principle of yin and yang. Light and dark are two halves of a whole. One cannot exist without the other. And more important, they are connected by infinite shades of gray."

Uh-oh. I was starting to see where this was going. I'd had similar conversations with Cal and with David Redstone. The whole point of this light/dark concept is that it isn't always crystal clear what belongs on which side. Making a choice for good isn't always easy or even identifiable.

"For example," Hunter went on, "a microbe can kill—like botulinum toxin. But the same thing, in a tiny amount, can be healing. A knife can be used to save a life or to take it. Love can be the most joyous gift or a strangling prison."

So true, I thought, thinking of what I'd lost with Hunter. I also couldn't help flicking my eyes toward Sky. Her face was composed, she was looking at the ground, but at Hunter's words a delicate pink blush bloomed on her pale cheeks.

"The sun itself is necessary for life," Hunter said, "but it can also burn crops, make people die of thirst, sear our skin until blisters form. A fire, too, can bring life, make our food healthy, help protect us—but it can also be a raging avenger, consuming everything in its path, taking life indiscriminately, and leaving behind nothing but ash."

I swallowed, a mosaic of fire images dancing in front of me. Fire and I had a love/hate relationship. Fire and I had been close allies until Cal had tried to kill me with fire . . . and fire had been Ciaran's weapon against my mother.

"Light and dark," Hunter said. "Two halves of a whole. Everything we do, say, feel, express—it all has two sides. Which side to promote is a decision we each make every day, many times a day."

I felt like Hunter was speaking directly to me. The differences between light and dark, good and evil were simply blurred for me sometimes. Almost every experienced witch I had ever spoken to had confessed the same thing. The horrible thing was, the more you learned, the less clear it was. Which was why an unshakable inner compass of morality was so necessary. Which was what Hunter was trying so hard to help me develop.

I sighed.

After the circle Bree pulled out some sodas, seltzer, and munchies, and we fell on them. I often craved something sweet after making magick, and now I eagerly downed some chocolate-chip zucchini bread.

"This is delicious," Jenna said, taking a slice of the bread. "Did you make this, Bree?"

Bree laughed. "Please. I don't know how to work an oven. Robbie made it."

I avoided talking to either Hunter or Sky, and when people started going home, I nipped out the door to my car. I was exhausted and wanted to digest tonight's magick. I didn't want to talk or think about light and dark anymore. I wanted to go home and fall into bed. For the first time since my parents had left, I wished they were home, waiting for me. It wasn't that I hadn't missed them so far—but I hadn't felt a *need* for them. Tonight I knew I would have been comforted by their presence in the house.

As I pulled into my dark driveway, I wondered where Raven had been tonight. Had she blown off Sky because of their fight, or had she and Killian gotten together?

My chest felt heavy and my hands were cold as I went into the house. In my room I got ready for bed. With Dagda snuggled next to me, purring, I lay in the dark for a long time, thinking. Killian couldn't be trusted, not really. And Ciaran was getting closer with every breath.

It was a long time before I slept.

12. Ciaran

Thank you, Brother Colin, for your kind words and also the gift of wine you sent. I have added it to the abbey's cellar, and Father Josef was most appreciative. Thanks be to God, I am well, though still troubled by confusing visions and dreams. My knowledge of the Prussian language is expanding greatly, and I am in awe of the abbey's library of precious and holy books. They have amassed a glorious storehouse of religious works, and I believe they are most selective about with whom they share this wealth.

Here, living, working, and praying in silence, I feel that I am free from my troubles of the past.

—Brother Sinestus Tor, to Colin, April 1770

When I awoke on Sunday, I lay in bed until my head seemed clear. I wondered what my parents were doing and if they had church services on cruise ships. Surely they did. I wondered if Mary K. had found a Catholic church near their ski resort. Since I had discovered Wicca, my sister had thrown herself into Catholicism with a vengeance.

"Maybe I'll go to church," I said out loud.

Dagda sat on the kitchen table, where he was so not allowed, and washed a front paw. He looked at me with his solemn gray kitty face, his big green eyes. "I just *feel* like it," I told him, then went upstairs to get dressed.

My family has been going to St. Mary's all my life. It's like attending a family reunion. I had to talk to five people before I even sat down.

The thing about Catholicism is that it can be comforting. It provides a structure to live your life within. In Wicca everything is wide open: choices about good and bad, ideas about how to live your life, ideas about how you celebrate Wicca and all its facets. Nothing is really, truly set in stone. Which was why individual knowledge is so important, because each witch has to determine all these things for herself. The way I saw Wicca, it was more based on the individual's choices and beliefs and less based on a set of rules. However, along with freedom comes responsibility and the increased possibility of completely screwing up.

Today, as I sat and knelt and stood automatically, reciting words and singing hymns, I was able to see some of the things that Wicca and Catholicism shared. They both had days of observation, reflection, and celebration, according to the year's cycle. Some Wiccan Sabbats and Catholic Holy Days of Obligation coincided—noticeably Easter, which occurs at the same time in both religions, except we called it Ostara in Wicca. Both holidays celebrate rebirth and use the same symbols: lambs, rabbits, lilies, eggs.

Both religions used external tools and symbols: sacred cups, incense, prayer/meditation, robes, candles, music, flowers.

To me it offered a continuity that helped me make the transition from one to the other. I hadn't completely given up being a Catholic—I didn't truly see how I ever could. But more and more my soul was turning to Wicca. It seemed a path I couldn't go backward on.

The choir filed out, singing, their voices raised in one of my favorite hymns. Father Thomas, his censer swinging, walked past, followed by the cross and Father Bailey. When it was my pew's turn to leave, I fell in line. I felt pleased and calmed and was glad I'd be able to tell my parents I'd attended services today. The rest of the day stretched before me, open, and I began to think about what I should do.

I was almost to the doors when my gaze fell lightly on someone sitting in the last pew, waiting for his turn to exit. Then my heart stopped, and my breathing snagged in my throat. Ciaran. My father.

He saw me recognize him. Standing, he followed me as I left the church, passing through the tall, heavily carved wooden doors. My heart kicked into gear again and thumped almost painfully in my chest. This was my mother's soul mate: the one person meant for her to love and to love her. And they had loved each other desperately. But he'd already been married; Maeve wouldn't be with him, and so he had killed her.

Killed her. A cold knife of fear slashed through my belly. Ciaran could have killed me, too—hungry for my power, wanting to use it to strengthen Amyranth. I was entirely convinced that I was going to die at his hands until he had realized who I was and allowed Hunter to set me free and transport me to safety. Now we were going to meet again. What to expect? Should I be afraid now? How could we ever have a normal conversation?

Outside the church the sunlight hurt my eyes, and the daylight seemed harsh after the dim church. I smiled and nodded good-bye to several people, then took a left and walked around the side of the church to a small, winter-dead garden. Ciaran followed a few steps behind. When we were apart from everyone else, I turned back to him. My eyes drank him in, trying to see the person who had almost killed me in New York—and then had helped to save my life. Our eyes were similar; his hair was darker and flecked with silver. He was handsome and barely more than forty.

"My son contacted me," he said in his lilting accent, that deep, melodious voice that entered my bloodstream like maple syrup. "He said that he was here with you. I thought perhaps he had called me at your request."

"Yes," I said, trying to project courage. "He did. I met Killian in New York. I realized he and I were half siblings. I don't have any other siblings except your other children—not by blood." Mary K., please forgive me again. "I asked him to call you. I decided I wanted to know you because you're my biological father." All this was true, more or less. Very subtly I shut down my mind so he couldn't get in and projected an air of innocence and frankness.

His eyes on me were as sharp as snakes' fangs. "Yes," he said after a moment. "You're the daughter I didn't know about. My youngest. Maeve's daughter. Your coloring is more like mine, but your mouth is hers, the texture of your skin, your height and slenderness. Why didn't she tell me about you, I wonder?"

"Because she was scared of you," I said, trying to control the anger that was seeping into my voice. "You'd threatened her. You were married and couldn't be with her." *You killed her.* "She wanted to protect me."

Ciaran looked around. "Is there someplace we could go?"

I thought for a moment. "Yes."

The Clover Teapot had opened winter before last, on a little side street off Main. It was the closest thing we had to an English-style tea shop, and it seemed appropriate. Also, it was public and safe. I still wasn't sure what to expect from Ciaran. When we had ordered and sat at a small table by the front window, I felt his keen eyes on me again.

"Have you seen Killian?" I asked, playing with the handle of my teacup.

"Not yet. I will soon. I wanted to see you first."

We sat there, looking at each other, and I felt him cast his senses toward me. I shut him out gently, and his eyes widened almost in amusement.

"How long have you known you're a witch?" he asked.

"Four months, a little less."

"You're not initiated." It was a statement.

"No." I shook my head.

"Goddess," he said, and took a sip of his tea. "You know your powers are unusual."

"That's what they tell me."

"Who is your teacher? The Seeker?"

"Well, not really formally. It's hard because I also have regular school. And my parents don't feel comfortable with the whole Wicca thing," I surprised myself by saying. Ciaran was easy to confide in. I had to be on guard against that. Was he already spelling me, trying to get inside my mind?

"I can't believe any child of mine has to be concerned about such banalities," he said.

I sat there, trying not to look stupid. Despite having known about his coming, I felt ridiculously unprepared to deal with him, to have a conversation with him. How could I have a normal conversation with the man who had killed my mother, had tried to kill me? Only my sense of obligation to Starlocket and my affection for Alyce kept me from giving in to fear and getting the hell out of there. Did he already know I was working for the council? He knew Hunter and I were—had been—going out. Was he just playing with me before he struck me down?

"You should have grown up surrounded by gifted teachers who would have helped you develop your natural powers," he went on. "You should have grown up among the moors and rocks and winds of Scotland. You'd be unmatchable." He looked regretful. "You should have grown up with me and with Maeve." A spasm of pain crossed his face.

He was unbelievable. He had been *married,* had *seduced* my mother, then followed her to America and *killed* her because she wouldn't be with him. And Amyranth had no doubt been responsible for Belwicket's destruction! And now he was all upset because we hadn't been a happy little family. I looked down at my tea, numb with disbelief.

"I've asked people about you," he went on, and I almost choked on my lemon Danish. "I've found out surprisingly little. Just that Cal Blaire sniffed you out, revealed you to yourself, and then he and Selene tried to seize your power." His eyes were steady on my face. "And you resisted them. Did you help kill them?"

Blood drained from my face, and I felt almost faint for a moment. My anger fled. I had intended to control this interview, to lead him where I needed him to go, to get information out of him. What a naive plan that had been. "Yes," I whispered, looking out the lace-curtained window to the street outside. "I didn't mean to. But I had to stop them. They wanted to kill me."

"Just like you tried to stop me in Manhattan," he said. "Would you have killed me if you could? When you were on the table, knowing your powers were about to be taken from you—if you could have stopped it by killing me, would you?"

What kind of question was that? Would I kill him to save myself, when he had killed my mother, when I had never known him as a father? "Yes," I said, resenting his easy manner. "I would have killed you."

Ciaran looked at me. "Yes," he said. "I think you would. You're strong. Strong not only in your powers, but in yourself. There isn't anything weak about you. You're strong enough to do what needs to be done."

If he had been anyone else, I would have blurted how often I felt afraid, weak, incapable, inadequate. But we weren't really having a father-daughter chat. I needed him to give himself up to me.

"Do you still want to kill me, Morgan?" he asked, and the pull of his question felt like a tide, drawing me out to sea.

Resist, I thought. How to answer? "I don't know," I said finally. "I know I can't."

"That's an honest answer," he said. "It's all right. You must do what you can to protect not only yourself, but your beliefs, your way of life, your heritage. Your birthright. And it's amazing how often others want to impinge on these things."

I nodded.

He looked at me speculatively, as if wondering if I were genuine. I tried to relax, but I couldn't. My palms were sweating, and I rubbed them against my skirt. This was Ciaran, and as much as I wanted to take him apart and throw away the pieces, there was a part of me that still wanted to run into his arms. *Father.* How sick was that?

"Have you met witches who think badly about Woodbanes?" he asked.

"Yes."

"How does that make you feel?" He poured more hot water into his cup and dipped in the mesh ball filled with tea leaves again.

"Angry," I said. "Embarrassed. Frustrated."

"Yes. Any witch who can trace his or her heritage back to one of the Seven Great Clans has been given a gift. It's wrong to be ashamed of being Woodbane or to deny your heritage."

"If only I knew more about it," I said, leaning forward. "I know I'm Woodbane. I know Maeve was from Belwicket, and they were a certain kind of Woodbane. I know you're Woodbane, and you're different. Your coven in New York was totally different from the covens I've seen. I read things in books, and it's like everyone blames the Woodbanes for everything. I hate it." I spoke more vehemently than I had intended to, and when Ciaran smiled at me, I was startled by how it pleased me.

"Yes," he said, looking at me. "I hate it, too." He shook his head, watching me. "I'm proud of you, my youngest, unknown daughter. I'm proud of your power, your sensibility, and your intelligence. I deeply regret that I didn't see you grow up, but I'm glad I have the opportunity to know you now." He took a sip of his tea while I tried to get a handle on my emotions. "But do I know you?" he murmured, almost to himself. "I think I don't."

My breath stopped as I wondered what he meant, if he

was about to accuse me of trying to trap him. What could he do here, in the tea shop?

"But I want to change that," he said.

That night I found out that if you lie with your head flat on the open page of a textbook, you don't necessarily absorb knowledge any faster than if you read the words. God, it was impossible to concentrate on this stuff! What the hell difference did it make which general did what in the Revolutionary War? None of this made any difference in my life whatsoever. All it did was prove I could memorize, and so what?

The phone startled me from my history-induced coma, and I could tell immediately it wasn't Hunter. Eoife? I had already called to tell her about my tea with Ciaran, so it seemed unlikely that she would call again so soon. Killian? Oh, God, could I handle another marathon Killian party?

"Morgan?" The voice on the other end greeted me before I could even say hello, and it took me a second to place it.

"Ciaran?"

"Right. Listen, Killian and I are having dinner at a place called Pepperino's. Would you like to join us?"

My head felt foggy from too much studying. I tried to make sense of Ciaran's invitation. Dinner with my murderous father and unpredictable, charming half brother? Could I think of a better way to spend my Sunday night? "Sure, I'd love to. I'll be right there."

Pepperino's is an upscale Italian restaurant in downtown Widow's Vale. It has tuxedoed waiters, white tablecloths, and candles, and the food is incredible. My parents went there sometimes for a birthday or an anniversary. It was almost empty since it was late Sunday night, and the maitre d' led me to Ciaran's table.

"Morgan, welcome," said Ciaran, standing up. He shot Killian a glance, and Killian also stood up. I smiled at them both and sat down.

"We've just ordered," said Ciaran. "Tell me what you'd like. The waiter says the calamari ravioli is superb."

"Oh, no thanks," I said. "I already ate. Maybe just some tea?"

When the waiter came, Ciaran ordered me a cup of darjeeling and a slice of mocha cheesecake. I watched him, thinking how incredibly different he was from the father I had grown up with—my real dad. My real dad is sweet, vague, and slow to anger. My mom usually takes care of the money, the insurance, anything complicated. Ciaran seemed like he was always in charge, always knew the answer, could always come through. It would have been quite different, growing up with him. Not better, I knew, though we did seem to have a connection. Just different.

Ciaran and Killian were drinking wine that was a deep, dark purple-red. I detected the scent of crushed grapes and oranges and some kind of spice I couldn't identify. My mouth watered, and I wished I could have some, but I had sworn never to drink again for the rest of my life. I could almost taste the full, heavy flavor.

The waiter brought their appetizers and my cheesecake at the same time, and we all began to eat. How could I make this meeting work for me? I needed information. Thinking about this, I took a bite of cheesecake and smothered a moan. It was incredibly rich, incredibly dense, with notes of sour cream riddled with streams of sweet, smooth coffee and dark chocolate. It was the most perfect thing I had ever eaten, and I took tiny bites to make it last longer.

"Tell me about growing up here," said Ciaran. "In America, not knowing your heritage."

I hesitated. I needed to share enough to make him feel that I trusted him, yet also protect myself from giving him any knowledge he could use against me. Then it occurred to me that he was so powerful, he could use *anything* against me and my being on guard was a waste of time.

"When I was growing up, I didn't know I was adopted. So I believed my heritage was Irish, all the way through. Catholic. All my relatives are, all the people at my church. I was just one more."

"Did you feel like you belonged?" Ciaran had a way of cutting to the heart of a matter, slicing through smoke and details to get at the very core of meaning.

"No," I said softly, and took a sip of the tea. It was light and delicate. I took another sip.

"You wouldn't have fit in any better in my village," Killian broke in. His face looked rough and handsome in the dim light of the restaurant, his hair shot through with gold and wine-colored strands. He didn't have Ciaran's grace or sophistication or palpable power, but he was friendly and charming. "It was a whole town of village idiots."

I was startled into laughter, and he went on. "There wasn't a normal person among us. Every single soul was some odd character that other people had to watch out for. Old Sven Thorgard was a Vikroth who had settled in our town, Goddess knows why. The only magick he worked was on goats. Healing goats, finding goats, making goats fertile, increasing goats' milk."

"Really?" I laughed nervously. As hard as Killian was trying to entertain us, Ciaran was still watching us both with a suspicious, dark expression. I wondered whether that was his response to Killian or just evidence that he was actually planning to do away with the both of us.

"Really," Killian said. "Goddess, he was weird. And Tacy Humbert—"

At the mention of that name, Ciaran broke into a smile and shook his head. He drank some wine and poured a tiny drop more in Killian's glass. I relaxed a bit.

"Tacy Humbert was love starved," Killian said in a loud whisper. "I mean *starved.* And she wasn't bad looking. But she was such a shrew that no one would take her out more than once. So she'd put love spells on the poor sap."

Ciaran chuckled. "Her aim wasn't perfect."

"Perfect!" Killian exclaimed. "Goddess, Da, do you remember the time she zapped old Floss? I had that dog climbing all over me for a week!"

We all laughed, but I thought I detected a warning glance exchanged between Ciaran and Killian. I wondered what Ciaran's problem was. I loved hearing about the very different life Killian had lived in Scotland. "Here, top us up, Da," Killian said, holding out his wineglass.

With narrowed eyes Ciaran filled it half full, then put the bottle on the other side of the table. Killian gave Ciaran a challenging look, but being ignored, he sighed and drained his glass.

"Were there many Woodbanes in your village?" I asked.

Killian nodded, his mouth full. He swallowed and said, "Mostly Woodbanes. A couple of others. People on the outside of the village or who had married into families. My ma's family has been there longer than folks can remember, and they're Woodbanes back to the beginning."

At the mention of Killian's mother, a shadow passed over

Ciaran's face. He toyed with the last of his salad and didn't look at Killian.

"It must have been nice, being surrounded by people like you. Feeling like you fit in, like you belong," I said. "All celebrating the same holidays." Like Imbolc.

"It *is* nice to have an all-Woodbane community," Ciaran put in smoothly. "Particularly because of the commonly held view that most witches have about us. If it were up to them, we would be broken up and disbanded."

"What do you mean?" I asked.

"I mean, Woodbanes are like any other cultural or ethnic group who has been forcibly dispersed. The Romany in Europe. The Native Indians here. The Aborigines in Australia. These were intact cultures that other cultures found threatening and so were killed, separated, dispersed, exiled. Within the Wiccan culture, Woodbanes have been cast in that role. The other clans fear us and so must destroy us."

"How do you fight that?" I asked.

"Any way I can," he said. "I protect myself and my own. I've joined with other Woodbanes who feel the same way."

"Amyranth," I said.

"Yes." His gaze rested on me for a moment.

"Tell me about them," I said, trying to sound casual. "What's it like to have an all-Woodbane coven?"

"It's powerful," said Ciaran. "It makes us feel less vulnerable. Like American pioneers, circling their wagons at night to keep intruders out."

"I see." I nodded, I hoped not too enthusiastically. Maybe this was my chance, I realized. Ciaran was opening up. Talking about our Woodbane heritage seemed to animate him, to make him less suspicious. I remembered the sigil and thought if I could just touch his arm, in a loving, daughterly gesture, I might be able to quickly trace the sigil on his sleeve. . . .

"I'm glad to hear you say that," I said confidently, shifting my chair closer. "Woodbanes are persecuted, so it's only natural that we'd try to protect ourselves, right?" I smiled, and Ciaran only regarded me curiously. It was impossible to read that expression. Did he trust me? Trying to keep my hand from shaking, I lifted it from my lap. I will touch his hand and say thank you, I thought. Thank you for telling me that I shouldn't be ashamed of my heritage. I reached out to touch him. "Th—"

"Excuse me for a moment," Ciaran broke in, rising. He headed toward the back of the restaurant, and Killian and I were left alone. I was stunned. I moved my hand back to my lap. What was he doing? Had I been too obvious? Was he calling Amyranth to get help in capturing me again?

Ciaran had left his suit jacket folded over the back of his chair, and my eyes lit on it. If I could put the watch sigil on his jacket . . . But Killian's bright gaze stopped me.

"Do you have plans for Imbolc?" I asked quickly.

Killian shrugged, giving me an almost amused expression. Had he seen what I was thinking? "I'll hook up with a coven somewhere. I love Imbolc. Maybe I could sit in with Kithic."

"Maybe," I said evasively, wondering what Hunter's plans were for our celebration.

Ciaran was back in a few minutes and paid the check. I didn't sense any anger in his demeanor. He put on his jacket, and I regretted not tracing the sigil on it. What to do now? Should I press him for information? Goddess, I was bad at this.

"Morgan, can you come to the house where Killian's staying?" Ciaran asked as we left Pepperino's. "It's the house of a friend who's currently out of the country. She's been kind enough to let him stay there."

As I looked at Ciaran, trying to remain calm, terror gripped at my insides and refused to let go. This was the perfect opportunity to learn more about their plans and to plant the watch sigil. Yet the thought of actually being with Ciaran and Killian was beyond terrifying. What if he'd seen what I'd been trying? What if he was leading me back to the house to punish me for it?

"I got a glimpse of your remarkable powers in New York," he continued. "I'd like to see how much you know and teach you some of what I know. I'm impressed with your gifts, your strength, your bravery."

My glance flicked to Killian, who was carefully blank-faced.

He could kill me, I thought with a sick certainty. He could finish the job he was planning to do in New York. I tried hard to fight my fear—wasn't this what I'd been praying for all those party nights with Killian?—but my terror was too strong. I could only think about getting out of there.

I was hopeless. As a secret agent, I was a fraud.

"Gosh, I really can't," I said lamely, hoping I didn't sound as terrified as I felt. "It's late, and I've, um, got school tomorrow." I tried to produce a convincing yawn. "Can I take a rain check?"

"Of course," said Ciaran smoothly. "Another time. You have my number."

Another time. I gulped and nodded. "Thanks for dessert."

13. Comfort

Brother Colin, I am sure you will be most distraught to learn that I have received a letter from her. The abbot of course reads my post, and I cannot imagine he would let a missive from her pass, so perhaps the letter was spelled. (Do not think this to be my insensate fear—I am quite certain that the villagers of Barra Head had powers beyond what I as a mortal can comprehend.)

Naturally once I realized who it was from, I turned it over to Father Edmond and have since been praying in the chapel. But I could not stop myself from reading it, Brother Colin.

She wrote that she has been living in Ireland, in a hamlet called Ballynigel, and that she was delivered of a girl child at summer's end last year. The child, she says, is sturdy and bright.

I shall pray to God to forgive her sins, as I pray for forgiveness of mine.

She intends to return to Barra Head. I do not know

why she continues to torment me. I do not know what to think and fear a return of the brain fever that so weakened me two years ago.

Pray for me, Brother Colin, as I do for you.

—Brother Sinestus Tor, to Colin, October 1770

"All right, class," said Mr. Alban. "Before we start on 'The Nun's Tale,' I'd like you all to hand in your compositions. Make sure your name is on them."

I stared at my English teacher in horror as my classmates began to bustle purposefully, pulling out their compositions. Oh, no! Not again! I *knew* about this damn composition! I'd picked out my topic and done some preliminary research! But it wasn't due until . . . I quickly checked my homework log. Until today, Monday.

I almost broke a pencil in frustration as everyone around me handed up their papers and I had nothing to hand in. I was seriously screwing up. I had zero excuse except that my life seemed to be about more important things lately—like life or death. Not Chaucer, not compositions, not trig homework. But actual life, the life I would be leading from now on. I had five days until Imbolc.

The rest of the day passed in a drone. When the final bell rang, I went outside and collapsed on the Killian-less stone bench, feeling very depressed. I was confused; it was hard to focus; I felt like a horse was standing on my chest. I couldn't even summon the mental or physical energy to go home and meditate, which usually pulled all my pieces together.

"You look beat," Bree said, sitting next to me.

I groaned and dropped my head into my hands.

"Well, Robbie and I are going to Practical Magick," she said. "Want to come?"

"I can't," I said. "I should go home and study." Actually, I would have loved to have gone, but it seemed likely that Ciaran was keeping tabs on me. I didn't want him to have a chance to suspect I was working with Alyce on anything. There was only a handful of days before Imbolc. I felt the clock ticking even as I sat there.

As the Kithic members drifted off, I felt sad and alone. My miserable failure last night weighed heavily on my conscience. If I had had the guts to go with Ciaran, who knows—I might be done with the mission by now. I had spent the entire day kicking myself, yet the memory of my terror was so real. I understood why I had refused to go; I just wished that somehow I could conquer my fear.

Across the parking lot my sister waved at me as she and Alisa got into Jaycee's mom's minivan. I'd talked to her this morning—she'd had a great time skiing.

I missed Hunter with a physical pain. If only he could be right by my side during this whole mission. I knew I had to see Ciaran and Killian again. I had to find out the exact time of the dark wave and possibly some of the spell words. I had to try to put a watch sigil on Ciaran. Part of me actually wanted to see them again, despite my mistrusting them and my deep-seated fear of Ciaran. They drew me to them because we were related by blood. Oh, Goddess. What to do?

The honk of a car's horn made me jump. Hunter's Honda glided to a halt next to me, and the passenger door opened.

"Come," he said.

I got in.

We didn't speak. Hunter drove us to his house, and I followed him up the steps and inside. Neither Sky nor Eoife was there, and I was grateful. In the kitchen Hunter still didn't speak but starting frying bacon and scrambling eggs. It occurred to me how hungry I was.

"Thanks," I said as he put a plate in front of me. "I didn't even know I was hungry."

"You don't eat enough," he said, and I wondered if I should take offense. I decided I would rather eat than argue, so I let it go.

"So," he said. "Tell me what's going on."

Once I opened my mouth, everything poured out. "Everything is so difficult. I mean, I like Killian. I don't think he's a bad guy. But I'm spying on him and using him. I think that Ciaran mistrusts me, but he also seems to—to care about me. And I'm completely terrified of him and of what he tried to do to me, what he did to my mother, what he's done to others. But I wonder how this is going to end. I mean, I'm going to betray both of them. What will they do to me?"

Hunter nodded. "If you weren't feeling these things, I'd be bloody worried. I don't have any answers for you—except that the ward-evil spells you know are more powerful than any you've worked before. And the council—and I—are going to protect you with our lives. You aren't alone in this, even if you feel that way. We're always with you."

"Are you following me around?"

"You're not alone," he repeated wryly. "You're one of us, and we protect our own." He cleaned his plate, then said, "I know

Ciaran is incredibly charismatic. He's not just a regular witch. From the time he was a child, he showed exceptional powers. He was lucky enough to be trained well, early on. But it's not only his powers. He's one of those witches who seems to have an innate ability to connect with others, to know them intimately, to evoke special feelings in them. In humans this kind of person, if they're good, ends up a Mother Teresa or Gandhi. If they're bad, you get a Stalin or an Ivan the Terrible. In Wicca you get a Feargus the Bright or a Meriwether the Good. Or, on the other side, a Ciaran MacEwan."

Great. My biological father was the Wiccan equivalent of Hitler.

"The thing is," Hunter went on, "all of those people were very charismatic. They have to be to influence others, to make others want to follow them, to listen to them. You're confused and maybe scared about your feelings for Ciaran. It's perfectly natural to have those feelings. You're related by blood; you want to know your father. But because of who he is and what he's done, you're going to have to betray him. It's an impossible situation and one that I didn't want you to take on, for just these reasons."

Hearing him imply he didn't think I could handle it made me want to insist I could. Which might have been why he said it. "It's not just that," I said. "It's other stuff. I mean, I like the way he talks about Woodbanes. Everyone else hates Woodbanes. I'm sick of it. I can't help who I am. It's a relief to be around someone who doesn't feel that way."

"I know. Even being half Woodbane, I catch that sometimes." Hunter cleared our places and ran the water in the sink. "A lot of that is old-fashioned prejudice from people who just don't know better. But covens like Amyranth do tend to set us back hundreds of years. Here's a group of pure Woodbanes who feel justified to murder and pillage other covens simply because they're not Woodbane. One coven like them can ruin things for the rest of us for a long, long time."

He was talking about the awful things Ciaran had done, and the thought of all the people he had killed made me shiver. My father was a murderer. I was *right* to be scared to be alone with him. In the end, Hunter hadn't made me feel better—but I didn't know if that had been his intention in the first place. He drove me back to school, to my waiting car, as silent as he had been on the ride to his house.

"Morgan," he said as I started to get out. I looked at him, at the glitter of his green eyes in the dim glow of the dashboard lights. "It's not too late to change your mind. No one would think worse of you."

His concern made my heart constrict painfully. "It *is* too late," I said bleakly, grabbing my backpack. "*I* would think worse of me. And if you're honest, you'll admit that you would, too."

He said nothing as I swung out of the car and headed for Das Boot.

14. Father

Brother Colin, you would hardly recognize me. I have lost almost three stone since last autumn. I can neither eat nor sleep. I have given up on myself; I am lost. God has chosen that I should pay for my sins on earth as well as in the burning fires to come.

—Brother Sinestus Tor, to Colin, February 1771

On Tuesday morning when I got in Das Boot to go to school, I found a book on the front seat. I was sure I had locked the car the night before. I'm the only person with a key. With a sense of foreboding, I climbed into the driver's seat and picked up the book. It was large and bound in tattered, weather-beaten black leather. On its cover, stamped in gold that was now almost completely flaked off, was the title: *An Historical View of Wodebayne Life*.

I turned the book this way and that and flipped through crumbling pages the color of sand. There was no note, nothing to say where this had come from or why. I closed my eyes for a moment and spread my right hand out flat on the cover. A thousand impressions came to me: people who had held the book, sold it, stolen it, hidden it, treasured it, left it on their shelf. The most distinct impression, no more than a fluttery butterfly-soft trembling, came from Ciaran. I opened my eyes. He had left this book for me. Why? Would having this book spell me somehow? Was it a no-strings gift or a devious trap? I had no clue.

At school I joined Kithic on the basement steps. Alisa was there, which was unusual, so I made a point to say hi.

I didn't mention the book, which I had just barely squeezed into my backpack, but sat down as Raven informed us all that she and Sky had broken up.

"It just wasn't working, you know?" she said, popping her gum in an ungothlike manner. "She couldn't accept me for who I am. She wanted me to be as dull and serious as she is."

"I'm sorry, Raven," I said, and I was. Raven had seemed a little softer, a little bit more happy, when she and Sky had first gotten together. Now she seemed so much more like her old self: cold, calculating, uncaring. I wondered if my bringing Killian to town had been the thing to finish off their relationship or whether it would have crumbled on its own. I couldn't decide.

"Yeah, well, don't be," she said, shrugging. "I'm glad to be out of it." She almost sounded sincere. But when I cast out lightly with my witch senses, I felt a surprising level of pain, sadness, confusion.

I waited for someone to mention Killian or to ask Raven pointed questions about him, but to my relief, no one did. I was pretty sure Killian had a lot to do with this breakup, whether or not he realized it or cared.

When the bell rang, I lugged my backpack to homeroom, feeling the book calling to me to read it. In English class I had a chance to and opened it up under my desk. It was written in old-fashioned language and had no copyright date or publishing info. The type was hard to read, which made it slow going. But after the first page I was hooked. It was fascinating. As far as I could tell, it was a nonfiction account of a monk's life, back in the 1770s. He had been sent to a far-off village to bring God to the pagans. I could barely take my eyes away from the pages and wondered why Ciaran had wanted me to read it.

I managed to escape detection through the whole class, and when the bell rang, I sneaked it back into my backpack and went up to Mr. Alban.

"Morgan," he said. "I seem to be missing your composition. Did you forget to turn it in?"

"No," I admitted, embarrassed. "I'm sorry, Mr. Alban—I spaced it. But I wanted to ask if I could do a makeup paper—maybe six pages long instead of four? I could turn it in next Monday."

He looked at me thoughtfully. "Ordinarily I would say no," he said. "You had plenty of time to do this paper, and every other student managed to turn it in on time. But this is unusual for you—you've always been a good student. I tell you what—turn in six pages, double spaced, on Monday, and we'll see."

"Oh, thanks, Mr. Alban," I said, relieved. "I absolutely will turn it in. I promise."

"Okay. See that you do."

I trotted off to calculus, already planning my outline.

* * *

Morgan. The power sink.

I looked up, though I knew I wouldn't see Ciaran.

"Morgan?" asked Bree. "What is it? You were in the middle of telling me about Mr. Alban."

"Oh, nothing." I shook my head. "Yeah, so he's letting me do a makeup paper. It's going to be cool, and this time I won't forget."

I sent a message back. *Tea shop?*

Fine, Ciaran responded.

"I said, do you want to go to the mall tonight?" Bree repeated patiently. "We could grab something to eat, shop, get home early."

"That sounds good," I said. "But I can't. Homework."

"Okay. Some other time." Bree walked toward her car, her fine dark hair being whipped by the wind.

On the way to the Clover Teapot, I tried to concentrate on my mission. Four days remained. It was still possible. I needed to get more information out of Ciaran. I needed to plant the watch sigil on him. I'll do it, I promised myself. Today is the day. I will accomplish my mission.

When I got there, Ciaran was already sitting at one of the smaller tables. I ordered and sat down, once again looking at him closely, seeing myself in him, seeing the possibilities of who or what I could have been or might still be. If I had grown up with him as my teacher, my father, would I now be evil? Would I care? Would I have almost unlimited powers? Would it matter?

I felt him looking at me as I took a sip of Red Zinger tea, holding the paper cup to warm my fingers. I needed a good opening. "Is it true that kids in Killian's village don't have to go to school?"

"Not to a government school," he said. "The village parents get home-schooling certificates. As long as the children can pass the standard tests . . ." He shrugged. "They can read and write and do sums. It's just that all the indoctrination, the governmental oppression, the skewed view of history—they don't get that."

"How much did you teach Killian, and Kyle, and Iona?" Killian had told me the names of his siblings. My other half brother, my half sister.

A troubled look clouded Ciaran's face, and he looked out the window into the thin, pale winter sunlight. "Is there somewhere else we could talk? More private? I had mentioned the power sink. . . ."

"I have an idea," I said. I stood up and gathered my cup of tea and a scone in a napkin. "I could show you our park." I acted like his agreement was a given. I couldn't go to the power sink, knowing that any magick he worked there would be dangerously enhanced. But if I were driving, if I chose the place—though really, these were only superficial reassurances. Ciaran was so strong that there wasn't much I could do to protect myself from him except work the ward-evil spells Eoife had taught me and hope for the best. But I was almost glad to be spending time with him. When we were apart, I was both scared and intensely curious about him. When I was actually with him, my fears danced around the periphery of my consciousness, and mostly I just soaked up his presence.

"Lead on," he said, and fifteen minutes later I parked Das Boot next to a Ford Explorer at the entrance to our state park.

We sat and drank our tea and ate our scones in silence. It wasn't an uncomfortable silence. But I had noticed that most witches were more peaceful to be around than most regular people. It was as if witches recognized the value of silence—they didn't see a lack of noise as a vacuum that needed to be filled.

"So how much did you teach Killian, Kyle, and Iona?" I repeated.

"Not very much, I'm afraid," was his quiet reply. "I wasn't a good father, Morgan, not to them, not by any stretch of the imagination."

"Why?"

He grimaced. "I didn't love their mother. I was tricked into marrying her because my mother, Eloise, and Grania's mother, Greer MacMuredach, wanted to unite our covens. I was just eighteen, and Grania got pregnant, and they promised me leadership over the new, very powerful coven. I would inherit all their knowledge, my mother's and Grania's."

I knew he was lying about being tricked into marrying Grania, but I played along. "Why would you inherit and not Grania? I thought lines were usually matriarchal."

"They usually are. But by the time Grania was eighteen and had been initiated and all the rest, it was clear that she lacked the ambition, the focus, to lead a coven. She wasn't really interested." His words were tight with derision, and I felt sorry for Grania. "But I was amazingly powerful. I could make the coven something new and stronger and better."

"So you married her. But she was pregnant. She didn't get pregnant by herself," I pointed out primly.

Ciaran's body tightened with surprise, and he looked at me as if trying to look through my eyes to something farther in. Then he threw back his head and laughed, an open, rolling laugh that filled my car and seemed to make the darkening twilight brighter.

I waited with raised eyebrows.

"Maeve said the exact same thing," he said. Saying her name, he grew more solemn. "She said the same thing, and she was right. As you are. My only excuse is that I was an eighteen-year-old fool. Which is not much of an excuse and not one that I've ever accepted from Killian. So I have a double standard."

His frankness was disarming, and I tried to picture him as a teenager. A very powerful Woodbane teenager. I had to lead him back to my question about Imbolc.

"Then I met Maeve," he went on, and his voice took on a richer timbre, as if even remembering his love made his throat ache with sadness. "I knew almost instantly that she was the one I should be with. And she knew it about me. Her eyes, the wave of her hair, her laugh, the shape of her hands—everything about her was designed to delight me. We were drawn to each other like—magnets." He looked at his own hands, fair skinned, strong, and capable. The hands that had set my mother on fire.

I desperately wanted to hear more, more about her, about them, about what had gone so terribly wrong. But I struggled to keep my focus on Starlocket. I had to put other needs before my own.

"Imbolc is coming up," I said. "Are you going to celebrate with Amyranth? Is Amyranth the coven you inherited from Greer?"

The inside of my car became very still. We kept our gazes on each other, each of us measuring, waiting, judging.

Then Ciaran said, "Amyranth is part of the coven I inherited from Greer. Not entirely—not everyone from Liathach wanted to join. And Woodbanes from other covens have joined us. But for the most part, those are people I grew up with, who I'm related to, who I can trust with more than my life." His words were soft, his voice like warmed honey. "We share blood going back thousands of years," he went on. "We're intensely loyal to each other."

"Like the Mafia?" I said.

Again he laughed.

Still, I found his description oddly compelling. The idea of being among people who were completely accepting and supportive, who only wanted to help you grow and increase your powers, whom you could trust implicitly, no matter what—it would be amazing. That picture of a Woodbane clan was too painful to think about—I could almost taste my own longing for it, and it terrified me to know that I was thinking about Amyranth. The coven that had tried to kill me. The coven that right at this moment was planning to destroy Starlocket. From the inside, I realized, it might not feel evil at all.

No one in my life had ever accepted me exactly the way I was. I didn't fit in as a Rowlands. Within my coven I stood out because I was a strong blood witch, and it had become clear to me that not even Robbie and Bree, my closest friends, could feel entirely comfortable around me anymore. Hunter and Sky and Eoife all seemed to want different things of me, for me to be different somehow, to make different choices.

My glance flicked back to Ciaran. How far could I push this? Was this the time to ask about the dark wave? Surely he suspected I was up to something.

"You're nervous," Ciaran said softly. "Tell me why."

It was dark now, and somehow there in the car I felt safe. "I'm incredibly drawn to that picture of Woodbanes," I told him honestly. "But I hated Selene Belltower and everything she stood for. She tried to kill me, and I know she had murdered others. I don't want to be like that."

He waved his hand in dismissal. "Selene was an overambitious, overconfident climber—in no way did she represent what my coven is about."

"What is your coven about?" I asked clearly. "I saw what you were doing in New York. What was that? Is there some larger plan?"

Ciaran sat back against the passenger door. His eyes on me were bright in the darkness, his powerful hands still on the wool of his coat. Slowly, slowly, his lips parted in a smile, and I saw his white teeth and his eyes crinkling.

"You are very interesting, Morgan," he said quietly. "You are a wild, untamed thing with the power of a river about to overflow its banks. Are you afraid of me?"

I looked at him, this man who had helped create me, and answered truthfully, "Yes and no."

"Yes and no," he repeated, watching me. "I think more no than yes. Yet you have every reason to be terribly afraid of me. I almost took your life."

"You almost took my magick—my soul—which is much worse than taking a life," I retorted. "But you didn't because you're my father."

"Morgan, Morgan," he said. "I find you very—gratifying. My other children are afraid of me. They don't ask me hard questions, they don't stand up to me. But you . . . are something different. It's the difference between a child born of Grania and a child born of Maeve."

Frankly, I was feeling kind of sorry for all of us, his children.

"You alone I see as being able to appreciate my coven," he

went on. "You alone I feel would understand. There's something being planned—"

I caught my breath silently, willing him to continue. He stopped and looked out the window, as if he hadn't intended to say so much. "I really should be getting back," he said absently.

I squelched my disappointment and frustration. It would be too easy for him to pick up on them. Without a word I started my car and backed out of the parking space. We drove back through the night, toward town. I tried not to even think about what he'd almost said, what we'd talked about. There would be time enough for that later.

I drove Ciaran back to where he said Killian was staying. The house was nowhere near the deserted road where Killian had had me drop him off. He must have been out—the house was dark.

"Good-bye for now," he said. "But not for long, I hope. Please call me soon."

I nodded and leaned closer. In a low voice I said, "Father, I want to do what you do. I want to work how you work. I want you to show me."

He shut the door, his face flushed with emotion at the word *father.* I drove off without looking back and cried the whole way home. I had called him Father. I hated myself.

15. Persecution

Brother Colin, by now you will have heard of my latest travail. Why God has chosen this fate for me, I do not know. All I can do is submit to His will.

I arrived in Barra Head ten days ago. Father Benedict had changed hardly at all and welcomed me most lovingly, which brought tears to my eyes. The abbey had changed for the better, with glass windowpanes, a pigsty, and two milk cows. The brothers (there are now eight) were planning the solemn celebration of Easter, our Lord's rising, with the handful of villagers who share their worship.

Between matins and laud, I left my cell and headed for the village in the darkness. I do not know what my thoughts were on that sole, dark walk, but with no warning I was knocked to the ground and a sleek black wolf was ripping at my cowl, tearing at my shoulder. With God's grace I held off its attack for a moment, and what I saw in those few moments before I fainted can only be part of my insanity, I fear. When the moon struck this creature's eyes, I saw Nuala, looking out at me. Poor

Brother Colin, how you must pity me in my madness!

Now I am in hospital. I envy you, my brother, for having been spared this hellish existence. As soon as I am able to travel, I am being sent to the hospice in Baden.

—Brother Sinestus Tor, to Colin, March 1771

"So this was a good day," Bree said. She propped one booted foot up on the stone bench next to me. "It's not snowing, it's almost forty degrees, and I missed both trig and chemistry because of that fake fire alarm. Not bad for a Wednesday."

"Do we know who did the fire alarm?" I asked.

"I heard it was Chris Holly," Robbie said, coming up behind us. Chris was an ex-boyfriend of Bree's and a typical Bree castoff: good-looking in a jock kind of way, with the IQ of your basic garden toad.

"Oh, jeez," Bree groaned.

Robbie grinned. "Word is that he didn't study for his English and panicked. Unfortunately, he was observed pulling the handle."

I shook my head. "What a loser."

A muffled ringing sound overlaced their laughter.

"Your purse is ringing," Robbie told Bree, who was already taking out her phone. She said hello, hang on a minute, then handed the phone to me, mouthing, "Killian."

"Little sister!" came his cheerful voice. "I haven't seen you in days! How are you?"

"I'm fine," I said, smiling at the sound of his voice. "What have you been doing?"

"This and that," he said lightly, and I mentally groaned,

wondering what mischief he'd been causing. "Want to get together tonight? Maybe all the gang?"

"Yeah, let's get together," I said, walking a few paces away from my friends. "But can it be just you and me? I want some time to hang out and talk."

"Sure," said Killian. "Alone's fine, too. Let's meet at that coffee place in that row of shops you took me to. We can decide what to do from there."

"Great," I said. "I'll see you there at eight tonight." I hung up and gave Bree back her phone.

"Okay, I'm gone." Robbie kissed Bree on the cheek and took off, not noticing how virtually every female around turned to look at him.

Bree watched him till he got into his red Volkswagen Beetle. "You do good work," she said, referring to the fact that Robbie had once been incredibly unattractive and now looked like a god, thanks to a little spell I had done. It had had unintended effects. Another lesson for me.

"How are things with you two?" I asked.

"Up and down," she said, clearly not wanting to talk about it. "What about you? How are you doing with your parents out of town, broken up with Hunter, and with a bunch of new relatives you hadn't known about?"

For a long moment I looked at Bree. Until four months ago I had known her as well as myself. But now we each had big secrets, unshared things between us. And I couldn't share this with her—about my mission, about my imminent betrayal of Killian and Ciaran, about my fear of being inevitably pulled toward dark magick.

"It's been up and down," I said, and she smiled.

"Yeah. Well, see you later. Call if you want to get together."

"I will," I said.

At eight o'clock I walked through the door of the coffee place that Killian and I had agreed to. I ordered a decaf latte and a napoleon.

An hour later I was royally pissed and rehearsing how I would blast him when he finally did drag his ass through the door. Except that I wouldn't be here to blast him because I was going home. I stomped outside to Das Boot and opened my door, only to see Raven's battered black Peugeot pulling up next to my car.

"Where's your friend Killian?" she said through her open window.

"He's somewhere being an hour late to meet me," I snarled.

Her eyes narrowed. "What do you mean? He was meeting *me*."

"Au contraire," I said. "We had an eight o'clock date."

"Well, princess," she said. "Your time is up. I've got him at nine. See ya."

I frowned. This was too strange. Why would Killian stand me up? What if he had messed up somehow, pissed someone off—had Ciaran done something to him? Or allowed someone else to do something to him?

I looked at Raven. "Will you do me a favor? Will you follow me to the house where he's staying?"

She frowned. "Why? He's supposed to meet me here, not at his place."

I gestured to the empty parking lot. "Do you see him? Besides, if he's on his way, we'll pass him and you can turn around. I just have a funny feeling about this."

Furrowing her brows, Raven gazed around the empty parking lot one last time. "All right," she said finally. "But if we pass him, we turn around and you go home."

"Deal." I climbed into Das Boot and headed out.

This was one of those times when I should have slowed down, thought things through, asked myself questions like, Is this smart? Am I likely to be killed or maimed doing this? Should I have some sort of backup plan? Any plan at all?

I screeched to a halt in front of the house where I knew Killian was staying. No cars were in the driveway, but the house was ablaze with lights, and even from out on the sidewalk I could hear music blasting. Raven and I looked at each other.

I rang the doorbell four times, but no one answered. Picturing Killian lying in a pool of blood, I used a little unlocking spell that Hunter had taught me and opened the door. The scent of incense drifted toward us. The house wasn't large, but it was old, and even I could tell it was beautifully decorated. A hundred candles of every color were burning in the living room. There was an open bottle of scotch on the coffee table and a couple of used tumblers.

Raven frowned, and I followed her glance. At the entrance of the hall leading to the back a black leather jacket lay on the floor. We walked over to it: a clue. My eyebrows rose. This jacket was Sky's—I recognized the silver pentacle hanging from her zipper. Together Raven and I, the unlikely duo, looked farther down the hall. I recognized Sky's black boots on the floor.

"What the hell?" Raven muttered, stalking forward.

Right next to Sky's boots was a man's belt. I thought I remembered Killian wearing it but wasn't sure. As if we were two puppets drawn on strings, Raven and I went forward. We came to a door that was slightly ajar. I heard the murmur of voices, and then good sense at last kicked in and I decided to get the hell out of here. Whatever Killian was doing, he was fine.

But Raven, not coming to this same conclusion, punched the door open with her fist. I knew it must have hurt, but not as much as the scene before us. Sky was sitting on the bed, and Killian was standing at the foot. They looked up in surprise when the door burst open, saw us, and started laughing. Killian was wearing only a pair of black pants. Sky was in a camisole and her underwear. My mouth dropped open in naive shock. Ridiculously, I remembered Hunter saying he didn't think Sky was actually gay—she just liked who she liked. Apparently right now she was liking Killian.

"Hi," Sky said, and laughed so hard, she almost fell sideways. She was drunk! I couldn't believe it. Killian, however, seemed a little more together.

"Little sister!" he said, and hiccupped, which made him laugh more. "Oops. I forgot our date, didn't I?" All around the room I could detect the faint traces of tingling magick, in the air, on the bed, on the floor. Goddess only knew what they'd been doing.

"And ours, too, you bastard!" Raven screeched, launching herself at Killian. He was unprepared and so went down heavily under her fury. She smacked the side of his face as hard as she could, and I winced as his head snapped to the side.

"Ow, ow," he said, but he was still laughing weakly.

"Oh, stawp, stawp," Sky was saying ineffectually in her slurred English accent. Leaving Raven and Killian rolling gracelessly on the floor, I went in search of a phone. Once I found it, I called Hunter.

"Come get Sky. She's smashed," I said, and gave him the address.

When I got back to the room, Raven was shrieking at Sky, Killian was on the floor, watching the scene with fascination, and Sky was starting to yell awful things back at Raven, personal things about their relationship that made my ears burn.

"Hold it!" I yelled, waving my arms. "Hold it!"

Surprisingly, the three stopped to look at me. I snatched up Sky's black leather pants and what I hoped was her shirt. Leaning over the bed, I grabbed her arm, hard. "You come with me," I said firmly, and she actually did, practically falling off the bed.

I dragged her out into the hall and down to the bathroom, where I shoved her roughly into her clothes. As soon as her arms were in the correct sleeves, I heard Hunter slam through the front door, shouting for Sky.

I produced her, handing him her boots and jacket.

At that moment the other two Stooges emerged from the bedroom. Raven's face was still contorted with fury, and Killian was starting to look a little less cheerful. Sky laughed when she saw him, and as Hunter began hauling her toward the front door, she yelled, "Go for it, Raven! He's a great kisser!"

I dropped my head into my hands. I was completely disgusted with all of them. Was everyone going completely insane? Looking at Raven and Killian with disdain, I left the house and went to see if I could help Hunter pour Sky into his car.

He was buckling her in. She looked tired and wasted but not unhappy. He turned to me, his face furious. "Are you happy with your charming brother now?"

My mouth dropped open. "I don't—"

"When is he going to learn to consider others?" he shouted. "Does he think it's a game, making magick in there, in this situation? Does he think it's funny to do this to Sky?"

I stood there, shocked, as he swung into the driver's seat and slammed the door. I knew he was upset about Sky, but I felt like he was blaming me for Killian's behavior. And I was the most blameless person in this ugly scene!

Futile tears of rage started coursing down my cheeks as Hunter peeled off into the night. I had given up the person I loved most just to prevent him from being tainted by my potential inherent evil, and here I was being blamed for my blood ties, even when I had nothing to do with their actions. I was risking my life to try to save Starlocket, and he thought I was cooking up party games with those three idiots.

Still crying, I was starting to cross the street to get to Das Boot when a car honked in my face and almost gave me a heart attack. I leapt back onto the curb in time to see a pimply-faced kid race past me in a souped-up muscle car. I watched him speed off, and as he did, he shot me the bird.

My mouth dropped open for the ninth time that evening. Without having one second to think, I raised my hand in a quick gesture and muttered just five little words. Instantly the kid's car locked up and he started skidding out of control, spinning sideways and heading right for the crash rail in front of a steep ditch. I was shocked.

"Nul ra, nul ra!" I said fast, and with another second the

kid had gained control of his car and come to a stop. After a moment he started the engine and continued down the road at a slower pace.

I sat down weak-kneed on the curb. What had I done? I had almost killed a stranger because I was upset at Hunter. I was unbelievable. Just last month I'd been involved in two deaths. What was wrong with me, apart from being Ciaran's daughter? Was this how my descent into evil would begin? After looking both ways I crossed the street and sat in my car. I cried for a long time, too upset to drive, and then I heard a voice, Ciaran's voice, saying, *Power sink.*

16. Shape-Shifter

I received your letter yesterday, and I thank you most gratefully. To answer your question, this hospice is not at all like a prison; as long as we stay on the grounds, we are allowed much freedom. There is no one here who is dangerous to himself or to another, though we are all tormented. I thank God that Father's estate can subsidize my stay here. They have allowed me to wear my monk's habit, and I am grateful.

I do not want to answer your other questions. Forgive me, Brother, but I cannot think on it.

—Simon (Brother Sinestus) Tor, to Colin, July 1771

The old Methodist cemetery was dark and cold, and a frigid wind whipped through the scrub pines and unshaped cedars that surrounded it. I strode forward, casting my senses strongly, and felt Ciaran waiting for me.

"Thank you for coming," he said in that soothing, accented voice. With no warning I burst into tears again, embarrassed to do it in front of him, and then his arms enfolded me; I was pressed against the rough tweed of his coat, and he was stroking my hair.

"Morgan, Morgan," he murmured. "Tell me everything. Let me help."

I actually couldn't remember the last time Dad had held me when I cried—I was too cool for that. I cried alone, in my room, quietly. Ciaran's embrace seemed so welcoming, so comforting.

"It's everything," I choked out. "It's being Woodbane and Catholic, it's having witch friends and nonwitch friends. It's Killian and Sky and Raven. Cal and Selene died, and I was so relieved, but I actually still miss Cal sometimes. Or the Cal I thought I knew." More sobs racked me, but still Ciaran held me, letting me lean on him. "And my folks are so nice and I feel like scum because I want to know my birth father!" I sobbed and wiped my nose on the back of my glove. "And I wish I had known Maeve, known her in person, but I *can't* because *you* killed her, you *bastard!*" My fist flew out quickly and slammed Ciaran in his chest. He swayed backward a bit, but I'd been too close to put much into the punch. I swung again, but he caught my wrist in a grip like a braigh and stilled me.

"I'm so sorry, Morgan," he said, his voice sounding torn. "I'm tortured about Maeve's death every day of my life. She was the best and the worst thing that ever happened to me, and not a day goes by that I don't feel pain and anguish over what happened. The only good thing about her being gone is that she can no longer feel pain; she's no longer vulnerable and can no longer be hurt."

I leaned backward into a tall tombstone and buried my face in my hands. "This is all too hard," I cried. "It's too much. I can't do it. I can't bear it." In that second all that felt absolutely true.

"No," Ciaran said, holding my wrists gently. "Yours is not an easy path. Your life feels hard and difficult now, and I can promise you it will only become harder and more difficult."

I made an indistinct sound of despair, and his voice went on, slipping into me like a fog.

"But you're wrong in thinking you can't do it, can't bear it," he said. "You absolutely can. You are Maeve's daughter and my daughter. You have our strength in you. You are capable of things beyond your imagination."

I kept crying, the tension of the past week spilling out of me into the dark night. Tonight's awful scene, all my conflicting emotions, were being dissolved in a salty wave of tears.

"Morgan," Ciaran said, brushing my hair out of my face. "I cherish you. You're my link to the only woman I've ever truly loved. I see Maeve in your face. And of my four children, you are the most like me—I see myself in you in a way I don't with the others. I want to trust you. I want you to trust me."

A chill shook me, and Ciaran rubbed my arms. Slowly my crying subsided, and I wiped my eyes and nose. "What happens now?" I asked him. "Are you going to disappear from my life, like you did with your other kids?" I saw Ciaran wince but went on. "Or will you be with me more, teach me more, let me know you?"

How much was true and how much manipulation to fulfill my mission? Goddess help me, I no longer knew. He hesitated, and a slow shivering made me tremble from head to toe.

At last he said, "You're young, Morgan. You're still gathering information. You don't need to make any life decisions today, tonight."

Gathering information? Chills ran up and down my spine. What did he mean by that? How much did he know?

I nodded slowly, unable to look in his eyes.

"What I would like you to do," he said, "to have, is a more complete understanding of what being Woodbane can mean—the joy, the power, the beauty of its purity, the ecstasy of its potential."

I looked up then, hazel eyes meeting hazel eyes. "What do you mean?"

"I would like to share something with you, my youngest daughter," he said. "You, who are so close to my heart and so far from my life. I sense in you something strong and pure and fearless, something powerful yet tender, and I want to show you what that could be. But I need your trust."

I was scared now and also unbelievably drawn to what he was saying. There was a taste in my mouth, and I licked my lips, then realized it wasn't actually a *taste* so much as a longing: a longing for what Ciaran was talking about.

"I don't understand." The words came out in a near whisper. "Is this about—"

"I'm talking about shape-shifting," he said quietly. "Assuming another being's physical form in order to achieve a heightened awareness of one's own psyche."

Suddenly I realized where he was going with this. I tried not to gape. I had heard about witches shape-shifting before—in fact, I knew that the members of Amyranth shape-shifted—but I understood that it was generally forbidden, considered dark magick. Of course, that wouldn't stop Ciaran.

"You're kidding, right?" I asked.

"No. Morgan, you have so much to learn about your own persona. You must trust me—there is no better way to know yourself than looking through another being's eyes."

"Shape-shifting? Like a hawk? Or a cat?" He couldn't be serious. Where was he going with this?

"Not necessarily a hawk or a cat," he explained. "No witch can change themselves or someone else into a being that does not resonate with the one to be changed. For example, if you feel an affinity for horses, want to know what it would feel like to race across the plains, then it's fairly easy to shift into that. But if you feel no affinity for the animal, have nothing of that creature in you, then it can't be done. Which is why witches don't usually shift into most reptiles or fish."

Oh, Goddess, he seemed serious. I tried to stall. "Can all witches do this?"

"No. Not even very many. But I can, and I think you can, too." He looked deeply into my eyes until I felt that the two of us made up the entire universe. "What do I feel like to you?" he whispered. "What do you feel like?"

An image came to me, an animal. I hesitated to say it. It was the animal that had come to me in terrifying dreams in New York—the animal that represented Ciaran and all of his children, me included. I was so scared about what might happen right here, right now, that it was beyond comprehension. But if I couldn't understand it, then I couldn't really feel it. "A wolf," I said. "Both of us."

His smile was like the moon coming out from behind a bank of clouds. "Yes," he breathed. "Yes. Say these words, Morgan: Annial nath rac, aernan sil, loch mairn, loch hollen, sil beitha . . ."

Mindlessly, wondering if I were being spelled by Ciaran but no longer caring, I repeated the ancient, frightening words. Before my eyes Ciaran began to change, but it was hard to say how—were his teeth sharper, longer? His hands curling into claws? Did I see a new, feral wildness in his eyes?

His voice was growing softer and softer, and I cast my senses out to hear the words so I could repeat them. Then I heard something that wasn't a word. It was . . . a sound and a shape and a color and a sigil, all at once. It was impossible to describe. No. It was Ciaran's true name, the name of his essence. I don't know how I recognized it . . . it was instinctive. I had learned Ciaran's true name, I thought hazily. That meant . . .

In the next second I gasped and bent double, racked with a searing, unexpected pain. I stared down at my hands. They were changing. I was changing. I was shape-shifting into a wolf. Oh, God, help me.

I cried out, but my voice was already not my own. I dropped to my hands and knees, feeling the soft loam beneath me, barely aware of Ciaran changing, slipping out of his clothes, revealing a thick black-and-silver coat. His intelligent hazel eyes looked at me from a wolf's face. I tried to scream in horror and pain, but my voice was strangled and broken. My body was in a rack, being forced to bend and curl in unnatural ways, as if every bone was being stretched or compressed or twisted in some incomprehensible nightmare. Helplessly whimpering, I closed my eyes and fell on my side, unable to fight or resist this overwhelming process. When Ciaran nuzzled me, I reluctantly opened my eyes again, and when I got up, it was on all fours. I was a wolf.

My fur was thick and russet colored. I looked down and saw four straight, strong paws tipped with sharp, nonretractable claws. I looked at Ciaran and recognized him: he was absolutely himself, yet he was a wolf. I felt absolutely myself, but as I began to cautiously examine my internal processes, I felt quite different. Foreign. Like a wolf instead of a person. It was as if my humanness was a rope hammock that had come undone on one end, and I was now watching it unravel. Soon it would be completely gone. I had two thoughts: How would I get it back? And what of my mission?

I stepped closer to Ciaran, my four legs moving smoothly, precisely, with no effort. I felt how strong I was, how powerful—my jaws felt heavy, my legs were roped with lean muscle, and I was breathing easily, although the change had been horribly stressful. Ciaran opened his mouth in a sinister, wolfy grin, as if to say, Isn't this great? I grinned back at him and was awash with a sudden ecstasy, an exhilaration that I was experiencing this. Instinctively I stepped closer to Ciaran and nuzzled his neck, and he returned it.

Then I remembered. The watch sigil. The wolf in me wanted to be running, to be away, to be coursing through the dark night. The last vestige of a human Morgan remembered the watch sigil. I pressed my face against Ciaran's thick neck fur and breathed the words of the spell against him. In a quick, desperate move I traced the sigil against his neck with my wet canine nose.

Ciaran made no response, as if he hadn't noticed, hadn't felt it. I had no idea whether it would "stick," since he was a changed being. Then Ciaran nudged me with his head and, turning, bounded off into the night. Feeling fiercely happy, all thoughts of Morgans and missions and spells gone, I leapt after him. My muscles contracted and expanded effortlessly; it was easy to catch up to him, and we loped along side by side as a million new sensations flooded my animal brain. With my magesight I could always see well in the dark, but now it was as if things were highlighted and outlined for me with infrared. With each indrawn breath a world of scents, flavors borne on the breeze, added an incredible depth and dimension to my experience. I felt incredibly powerful, agile, and surefooted. It was wonderful, beyond wonderful, exciting beyond description.

When Ciaran looked back, I opened my mouth and showed him my pointy teeth. He had given me the gift of a lifetime, I knew. We ran for miles through the woods, leaving the cemetery behind, following scents, feeling the crisp air ruffling through our fur. I ran happily in Ciaran's paw prints, trying to soak up as much of this sensation as possible. I didn't know if it would ever happen again, and I wanted to relish every second.

I hadn't even begun to tire when Ciaran cantered to a halt and sniffed the air. Eagerly I stood next to him, shoulder to shoulder, and lifted my head. My eyes widened, and I looked at him, seeing the knowledge in his eyes. I smelled it too. Prey.

17.
The Choice

Colin, I write to you in fevered hysteria. I learned only hours ago that Nuala is to be burned at the stake, in Barra Head. I can see that at last her devil's work has caught up to her, but the sentence! As Father Benedict himself said, God is to judge good and evil, not man! Cannot her soul yet be saved? Can no one bring her to the Lord's joy? It can be done only if she is alive—surely they must see that, Colin!

I have been insane with worry since receiving this news (news that I am sure I was not meant to know). My brain cannot comprehend her fate at the stake. And what of the child? I beg you, send to Barra Head and inquire. I know not the child's name, nor can I verify whether or not it still lives. But try, for my poor sake.

I will await the next post with all anxiety.

Simon Tor, to Colin, October 1771

Prey. Oh, God, I was hit by a hunger so strong, it almost overwhelmed me. It was a blood lust, an animal's need to kill or be killed, hunt or be hunted. I was a predator—an efficient, predestined killer—and the idea of prey made my stomach tighten in anticipation. I licked my lips and inhaled deeply, drawing the delicious scent into my lungs. It was almost familiar, a wonderful, maddening smell that I had to follow or die trying.

Without waiting for my father, I set off after the prey, my feet moving swiftly and silently over the detritus of the forest floor. Prey, prey, I thought. My prey. The scent swept through these woods, here touching a tree trunk, here brushed against leaves on the ground, here on the holly bushes with their shiny, prickly leaves. Sometimes the trail doubled back on itself, and I circled trees in frustration until I found the one thread that was a fraction newer, a fraction stronger. Then I was off again, moving like a wraith through the darkness, filtering out a thousand other scents: tree, loam, mold, bird, insect, deer, rabbit. But I focused only on the one scent, that one tantalizing smell that made my mouth ache in longing.

I was barely aware of the other wolf, the black-and-silver one trotting behind me; I couldn't hear his breathing, and his paws made almost no sound.

Here I took a sharp right, and at once the scent became closer, stronger. I almost howled in excitement. *Soon. Close. Mine.* The next second I froze: there it was! The scent was washing over me now, the air woven through with it. It was close. With every breath I inhaled the promise of the joy of victory over a lesser being. It was beyond hunger, beyond desire, beyond want. My mouth was wet; my eyes were piercing the night. I scanned the woods all around me as the other wolf came to a silent stop next to me. Tree by tree by tree by bush by bush . . . It was close. It was within range.

There! There, forty feet away. My moving target, my destination, my fate. It was heading away from me, leaving an obvious trail for me to follow. I smiled. Without having to think, my muscles gathered and exploded, launching me into the night. The distance between us closed rapidly. I felt an intense, palpable hunger, a need to bring my prey down, to sink my sharp white teeth into its flesh, to taste its fresh, hot, salty blood. I whimpered with want and raced ahead.

With one more leap I would bring it down. My weight would knock it to the ground; it would be scared, confused; I would rip into its throat and not let go. . . . The prey turned and saw me rocketing toward it. Then it was on the move, charging away from me, running in zigzags, ducking below branches, crashing through the underbrush with as much noise as a tree falling heavily to the ground.

I chased after it, following the traces of its warm footprints, its scent, now laced with fear, that it left in its wake. My breath came rapidly, my lean sides pumping oxygen efficiently through my blood, my incredibly strong heart pushing fresh blood through my veins.

I was glad my prey was putting up a chase—it shouldn't be too easy. I felt the other wolf behind me, and I sensed that he was enjoying this as much as I was. I detected a familiarity in his movements: he had done this before. Hunted before. Killed before.

A streak of crackly blue light flew through the trees and almost hit my head. I ducked instinctively, and it exploded on a pine next to me. The scent of charred bark and sticky-sweet sap hit my nostrils. Another ball of blue light came at me, and once again I dodged, almost feeling annoyance. I hunkered down, kept my head low, and concentrated on following my prey.

A strong scent of deer crossed my path, and it would have made me swerve if I had been after any other animal. The air seemed full of delicious scents: deer, rabbit, turkey—but I ignored them, as I ignored the false, confusing trails that told me my prey had taken another path. I was unstoppable, undistractable. I had one purpose. I knew what I wanted, and I wanted it more than I'd ever wanted anything in my whole life.

The other wolf moved away from me, splitting off from my path and heading farther on. I realized he was going to come at our quarry from the left side, while I would chase it from the right. Together we would corner it, and then I alone would bring it down; I alone would get the spoils of victory.

Within a minute we had succeeded: there was a sharp rock outcropping here, and my prey was trapped against it. It flattened itself against the wall, as if that would help. The other wolf moved in, but I growled at him to stay back. This life belonged to me. I could hear it panting, gasping to get air into its puny lungs. The smell of fear covered it and made me wrinkle my nose. Its heart was hammering within its weak chest, and the thought of the blood pumping through that heart made me step closer, baring my teeth.

This was what I wanted more than anything. I had to bring it down, had to kill it, had to taste it. It was created solely to be my victim. The fur on my back stood up in a bristly line with excitement. Hunkering down, a low growl coming from my throat, I began to creep toward it. My eyes never left it, my muscles were poised to leap at any second if it should try to run. Its pale green eyes were wide with fear, and I wanted to grin.

Should I leap on it and drag it down, face first? Should I launch myself toward it from the side? How much could I play with it before it died? No, better to make a clean, quick kill. It was the wolf's way. Ever so slowly I advanced, feeling a delicious thrill flooding my being. Nothing was better than this sensation, this victory over weakness. Nothing could compare.

I glanced up and found that my prey was staring at me, right at my eyes. I frowned. That wasn't what prey did. Prey cowered, prey hid, prey made it fun. Prey didn't stare at its hunter. I took another step closer, and its gaze caught mine, unwavering. It was *infuriating*. I pulled my lips back to show it my deadly fangs; I growled deeply from within my chest, knowing that the vibrations of the rumble would strike terror into it. Closer and closer I went, becoming more enraged by the second by its boldness.

Then my prey whispered, "Morgan?"

I froze, one paw in midair. I blinked. That sound was very familiar. Behind me the other wolf stiffened, then moved closer, barely rustling the leaves on the ground. I turned my head a fraction and growled a warning to him: Stay back. This is my kill.

"Morgan?" My victim was still panting hard, sweating, pressed against the rocks. It looked deeply into my eyes, and with surprise I found it almost painful. I desperately wanted it to turn away, to quit staring at me. As soon as it dropped its gaze, I would leap on it, tearing out its throat, feeling its lifeblood soaking into my fur. Look away, I commanded it silently. Look away. Play your role, as I play mine.

It wouldn't look away. "Oh, Morgan," it said. With its next breath it straightened up, away from the rock, and my muscles tensed. Unbelievably I felt it relaxing, calming its fear. It raised its paws and unwrapped some covering from around its neck. My eyes opened wider—it had bared its throat for me! I could see pale, smooth skin where before there had been only some thick, wrinkly thing. "Your choice, Morgan," it said, and waited.

Again I blinked, trying to process this situation in my wolf brain. This wasn't making sense. This prey was talking to me, it was saying my name. My name? My name? I thought—I felt only like Me. But like a trickle of water slowly eating through rock, a realization got through to me. My name was Morgan. My name was Morgan?

Oh, Goddess, my name was Morgan! I was a girl, not a wolf, not a wolf! Only a girl. And my prey was *Hunter,* and I loved him, and right now I wanted to kill him and taste his blood more than anything in the world.

What was happening?

"Your choice, Morgan," Hunter said again.

My choice. What kind of choice? I had hunted him down; the right of the kill was mine. Could I choose *not* to kill him? Abruptly I sat down, my haunches folding neatly under me, brushy tail swishing out of the way.

My choice. I would choose what? To kill or not to kill? Oh, Goddess, was the choice between good and evil? Between power or guilt? Light or darkness? Oh, God, did this mean I couldn't kill this prey? I wanted it, I wanted it, I needed it, I had to have it.

Behind me the other wolf growled: Do something. Kill it, or I will.

Oh, God, oh, God, oh, Goddess, help me. Oh, God, I choose good, I thought, almost weeping with regret at the blood I wouldn't spill, the life I couldn't take. I threw back my head and howled, a strangled, smothered howl of pain and longing and a desire to kill.

And as soon as I thought, I choose good, my exhilarating wolfness began to slip away from me, like a tide away from a shore. This too I regretted: I wanted to be a wolf forever. How diminishing to go back to being a mere girl, a pathetic human; how pitiful, how humiliating! I lowered myself onto my front paws, wanting to weep but unable to: wolves can't cry.

The other wolf—Ciaran, it came to me—trotted forward suddenly with an irate snarl. Hunter tensed against the rock, and I leapt to my feet, thinking, No! No! I saw Ciaran's powerful muscles gather and knew he would be on Hunter in an instant. Quickly in my mind I thought his true name, the name that was his very essence, the name that was a sound, a shape, a thought, a song, a sigil, a color all at once.

Ciaran dropped in midleap like a stone. He turned to me, wolfish eyes wide with astonishment, awe, and even fear. No, I thought. You may not have Hunter.

Things began happening too quickly to comprehend. I began to change back into a human, and it was painful and I cried out. Ciaran, still a wolf, melted into the shadows of the woods like a fog, as if he had never existed. Then Eoife and many other witches I didn't know burst into the clearing, shouting spells and weaving magick everywhere.

"He went there!" Hunter shouted, pointing in the direction that Ciaran had gone. I lay curled on the ground, still mostly wolf, trying not to retch, knowing in my heart that they would never catch Ciaran, that my father had already escaped. But the weight of their magick and the strength of their spells amazed me—I didn't want to be anywhere near them. It was a weight, pressing on me, binding Woodbanes, chasing Ciaran, and the magick made me feel ill.

Vaguely I felt Hunter wrap me in something warm and pick me up, and then the pain of his every step was so much that I passed out and sank into a delicious darkness where there was no pain, no consciousness.

I don't know when I awoke, but when I did, I was stretched across Hunter's lap, wrapped in his overcoat. My eyes fluttered, and I whispered again, "I choose good."

"I know, love," Hunter whispered back.

I saw my naked feet sticking out from his coat; they were freezing. I felt impossibly pale and weak and wormlike after the glorious strength and beauty of wolfdom. I began to cry, thinking again, I choose good, I choose good, just in case it hadn't taken the first time. Hunter held me and stroked his hands over my bare human skin. He murmured gentle healing spells that helped take away the nausea and pain and fear. But not the regret. Not the anguish. Not the loss.

18. Imbolc

Diary of Benedict, Cistercian Abbot, December 1771

Today we held the sad burial and consecration of one of our sons. Brother Sinestus Tor was brought from Baden and laid to rest in the abbey's churchyard. His mother assured me he had received the last sacraments, but the brothers and I performed extra rites of purity and forgiveness. I cannot think that gentle Sinestus, so bright and full of hope, became an agent of the devil, but there are facts of this matter that trouble me greatly, though I shall take them with me to my own grave, God willing. How is it that the boy died at the exact moment of the exact day that the witch Nuala Riordan was burned at the stake? They were hundreds of miles apart and had no earthly communication. And what of the mark found on the boy's shoulder? His mother made no mention of it; I wonder, did she see his body or no? But the scars there cannot be explained unless he were burned. Burned with a star encircled on his shoulder.

I pray we have done the right thing by allowing him to rest in consecrated ground. May God have mercy on us all.
—B.

"Drink this," said Hunter, folding my stiff fingers around a warm mug. I took a tentative sip, then coughed, gagging on its foulness.

"Agh," I said weakly. "This is awful."

"I know. Drink it, anyway. It will help."

I did, taking small sips and grimacing after each one. If this tonic was magickal, why couldn't he have spelled it so it didn't taste like crap?

I was huddled in front of the fireplace at Hunter's house. He had given me some of Sky's clothes to wear since mine were back at the cemetery.

The fire crackled and spit in front of me, but I avoided looking at the flames. I couldn't bear anything else tonight—no revelations, no lessons, no visions, no scrying. Although I had a blanket wrapped around me, I shivered uncontrollably and felt that the fire put out hardly any heat.

I didn't understand anything.

"Is Sky here?" I thought to ask.

Hunter nodded. "Upstairs, sleeping off her drunk. Tomorrow morning she'll probably feel worse than you do now."

"I find that hard to believe." Every muscle and bone and nerve and tendon and cartilage in my body ached as if it had been torn. Even my hair and my fingernails hurt. I dreaded having to get up to walk, and driving seemed completely impossible. Creakily, like an old woman, I raised the mug to my lips and drank again.

"Why were you out there?" My words came out as a croak.

Hunter looked at me somberly. "I was looking for you. I got a message from Ciaran that you were in danger."

Ciaran. I don't know why I was surprised. "How did you know where I was? How did Eoife show up at the last minute?"

"We scried," said Hunter. "Ciaran had blocked himself from us, but you hadn't. Ciaran wanted us to look for you. He wanted to plant me in your path while you were shape-shifting. He was testing you."

I shuddered again at the thought of what I had almost done to Hunter. Then, considering Hunter's words, I frowned. "I did block myself. I was covered with protective spells, spells that wouldn't let anyone find me without my will."

For a moment Hunter looked uncomfortable, and I thought, Oh my God, he's lying to me.

"You have a watch sigil on you," he said, and blew out a breath, as though glad I finally knew.

"Ex*cuse* me?" I almost dropped my mug.

"You have a watch sigil on you." He looked embarrassed. "Since Eoife taught you the ward-evil spells. During one of those she put a watch sigil on you."

I stared at him.

"We needed to know where you were, who you were with. You're inexperienced, love, and that makes you a target. Any dark witch who knew that would be dangerous to you. There was nothing about this mission that was safe."

If we'd been having this conversation before Eoife had come to town, I would have been furious. As it was, after all I'd been through, all I knew, all I felt was a vague sense of gratitude. I sighed and murmured, "Take it off now."

"I will," Hunter promised.

I stared into the bottom of my dark mug. "I feel like such a failure. I haven't learned anything about the time of the dark wave, or the spell, or anything. I've sentenced Alyce and Starlocket to death." My eyes stung, and I knew tears would come later.

"No, Morgan," Hunter said, rubbing my knee through the blanket. "You got Killian here, and Ciaran. They know we're here and that we're on high alert. And you have to remember, you did incredibly well just to not have been killed."

"Oh, God." I groaned and shook my head. "At least I planted the watch sigil on him."

"What? You did?" Hunter looked incredulous. "When?"

"Right as we were turning, shifting. I breathed it into his fur and traced the sigil on his neck. Actually, that was probably useless, too. Once he changes back—"

"It will still be on him," Hunter said, his face breaking into a huge grin. "Oh, Goddess, Morgan! The council is going to be ecstatic to hear it. That's the best news I've had in a long time." He leaned and kissed my cheek and my forehead. "Morgan, I think your mission was a smashing success. You planted the watch sigil on Ciaran, and we're both still alive, unhurt. . . ." Hunter took my free hand and kissed it, looking at me encouragingly. I didn't know how to respond.

The truth was, his joy didn't affect me that much. I had planted a betraying sigil on my biological father. And he had given me such a gift. . . . For a moment I remembered running through the woods on all fours, and I closed my eyes.

And then I remembered . . . I had learned his true name. Ciaran's true name. Something that could give me complete power over my father, one of the darkest witches the world had ever known. The thought of using it against him made my stomach clench. For now, I thought, I would guard this as my secret. I wouldn't tell the council—wouldn't even tell Hunter. If it became necessary, I could use it. But I didn't want to give anyone else the power to destroy my natural father. I couldn't.

"He wanted you to kill me," Hunter said softly, as though he was reading my mind. He wrapped his arms around me, and I felt his warmth seeping through the blanket. "If you had killed me, it would have been one less Seeker—and you'd have lost your mùirn beatha dàn. It would have bound you to him in a way that love alone never could."

I shuddered at the thought of losing Hunter. "I was starting to care for him," I admitted.

"I know," said Hunter. "How could you not? He's your birth father. And I believe that his feelings for you were sincere also. Despite everything, I believe that's true."

Then I began to cry again, tears leaking silently out of my eyes and running hotly down my cheeks. I didn't have the energy to sob, and it would have hurt too much, anyway.

"I have you," Hunter said, holding me close. "I have you. You're safe. It's all right. Everything's going to be all right."

"There's no way anything will ever be all right again," I said shakily, and he began kissing the tears away from my cheeks.

"That's not true," he said.

I looked into his green eyes, the eyes that had stared me down when I was a wolf. And I knew then: I knew in my heart that I was good.

"I love you so much," I said.

He gave a half smile and leaned closer, blotting out my vision of the fire. He's going to kiss me, I thought, but by then his lips were already against mine. Tentatively at first, then with increasing pressure as I responded. Gradually I felt light growing all around us, bathing us in a silvery white glow. I reached one arm up to curl it around his neck, and then we had our arms around each other. We kissed deeply and more deeply, trying to fuse ourselves together after being apart too long. Then suddenly it was just like the day at Bree's house with Killian: flowers, all different kinds and colors and sizes, showering down upon us, petal soft. I broke away for a moment, gazing around me, and started to laugh. Hunter followed my gaze, looking up at the shower of petals, and his face transformed into a huge smile. He kissed me again, and his body pressed against mine, comforting me to my very soul. I held him to me as tightly as I could, all my muscles screaming in pain as I moved. I didn't care. I was back in Hunter's arms and he was in mine, and everything was going to be all right.

My parents came home the next day, while I was home "sick." I felt their car come up the driveway and quickly ran my hands over my ears, checking to make sure they were still round and naked instead of pointy and furry. Moving gingerly downstairs, I met them at the front door.

"Hi, honey!" Mom said, giving me a big hug. I tried not to moan in pain; every cell in my body still hurt. She glanced at her watch and looked at my face more closely.

"Morgan!" Dad said, struggling through the door with two suitcases. "Are you sick?"

"You look awful," Mom said, putting her hand to my cheek. "Do you have a fever?"

"I think so," I said. "I thought I'd better stay home today. It's the only day I've missed."

"Poor thing," Mom said, and I felt a maternal mantle of comfort settle around me. "You go get back into bed. I'll bring you some Tylenol and a ginger ale."

I almost wept with happiness. "I'm glad you're home," I choked out, then headed back upstairs to my waiting bed. Ciaran was gone, Killian hadn't been heard from since our father had disappeared, Hunter and I were back together (I thought), and my parents were home. It was a whole new day.

"Today is the feast of lights," said Eoife at our circle two days later. She raised a white candle high. "Today is for new beginnings, for purification, for renewal of spirit, body, hearth, and home. We give blessed thanks to the Goddess for the past year and dedicate ourselves anew to our studies and devotions."

Next to her Alyce Fernbrake ignited her candle from Eoife's, and the two women smiled at each other before Alyce turned and bent to light Suzanna Mearis's candle. Suzanna was now in a wheelchair. Around the circle went the flame, from candle to candle, witch to witch.

"Blessed thanks," we said when the last candle was lit. Then, moving deasil around Hunter and Sky's large circle room, we each sprinkled a small handful of salt on the floor around us. It crunched under our feet. I looked around at the many softly lit faces. It was Saturday night, Imbolc, February 2. For this joyful celebration, one of the four major Wiccan Sabbats, Kithnic had joined forces with Starlocket, and there were twenty-six of us purifying ourselves, this room, this year.

After Alyce had led us in a prayer to Brigid—she pronounced it Breed—the goddess of fire, we sat in a large circle. I gazed across at Hunter, thinking about how beautiful he looked in candlelight. He'd pretty much convinced me that after passing the test of choosing good over evil, I was probably safe for him to date. Now every time I looked at him, my heart went all fluttery and I wanted to hold him.

"Blessed be," Hunter said, and we repeated it. "This joyful occasion," he went on, "signifies the beginning of winter's end. The days are becoming longer, the sunlight brighter—it's a time of rebirth."

"Yes," said Eoife. "Many witches choose this time to spring clean their homes, performing purifying rituals and literally making a clean sweep of everything."

"It's also a time for spiritual rebirth," said Alyce, her wise face and blue-violet eyes serene. "I use this holiday to forgive anyone who wronged me in the past and to seek forgiveness from anyone I've wronged. To begin the new Wheel of the Year with a clean slate."

Alisa spoke. "I read there's a ritual where you write down things you wish to be free of in the coming year—flaws, problems, worries—and then you burn the paper."

"We will do that in a little while," Hunter said. "Right now let's stand again and call on the god and the goddess."

We all joined hands.

"May the circles of Starlocket and Kithic always be strong," Hunter said.

"Blessed be," I whispered. The other members murmured their response.

As we began to move widdershins in our circle, Hunter began to chant in a low voice. The chant was unfamiliar to me, but I understood it somehow: it was about new beginnings, casting the darkness behind you and living in light. Gradually Alyce and Sky joined in, and then the words came to me and I began to chant, too. Energy flowed through my body as we spun around the room. A joy began to fill me that cannot be put into words. We were all alive, safe. I caught Hunter's eye, and he smiled at me. He was mine again. My body filled with warmth and energy, and I smiled back.

On the other side of the circle Alyce's face was turned up in a mask of pure joy. I felt a rush of comfort. Alyce was still with me, and Starlocket was intact. I had helped make it that way. In the time to come, the council would track Ciaran, and if he should ever come for me again, I was ready for him. For the first time in weeks I felt utterly safe and happy.

I stared into the candle flames and felt my power rise.

Later that night, on my front porch, I fished my keys out of my jeans. My shoe tapped something, and I looked down. As soon as I saw the small, lumpy bundle of purple silk, my heart dropped. I whipped my head around, looking for Ciaran. I knew this was from him as surely as I knew I was a witch. I cast my senses out strongly and felt nothing except Dagda on the other side of the front door.

Slowly I knelt and picked it up. It was almost alive with tingling traces of magick. I untied the knot, and the bundle fell open. My mouth opened wordlessly as I stared down at the golden watch. It was the watch I had found in Maeve's old apartment in New York. Ciaran had taken it from me as he had tried to steal my powers. It was the watch that had first made him aware that I must be his daughter.

"Oh, Goddess," I muttered. A fluttering white note caught my eye, and I picked it up. *You should have this,* it said.

I stroked the watch, feeling the warmth of the gold, the

fineness of the wrought chain. This was truly a family heirloom, something to be kept and handed down for generations.

Unfortunately, it was also from Ciaran, which meant I shouldn't even be holding it. When Cal and I had first gotten together, he'd given me a silver pentacle necklace that I had worn constantly. It had been spelled, of course, and he'd used it to help control me. Goddess only knew what Ciaran had done to this watch: I knew he had given it to me sincerely, out of love, and I knew also that he'd had some ulterior purpose in doing so, that it would somehow be to his advantage. That was Ciaran: light and dark. Like me, like the world, like everything.

I tied it back into its purple silk. I desperately wanted to go inside and sleep, but instead I found myself sliding back behind the wheel of Das Boot. I drove well out of town, at least ten miles, to an old farm I had come to once with Maeve's tools. I walked through the tree buffer that separated the meadow from the highway and stepped into the clearing where Sky Eventide had found me, working magick on my own.

The ground was frozen, of course, but I'd come prepared and said a tiny spell that made digging easy. I dug a hole almost two feet deep and then with bittersweet feelings placed the purple silk bundle at the bottom of it. I filled in the hole. Then I knelt and said all the purifying spells I knew, all the ward-evils ones from Hunter and Eoife and Alyce. I stood up and made my way back to the car, feeling like I would be lucky to make it home without falling asleep at the wheel.

With time the earth's healing purity would work its own magick on the watch, purifying it and removing all traces of spells and evil. It would take a very long time. But one day, I knew, I would reclaim it.